THE WHEEL SPINS THIRTEEN

In Sharky Dexter's casino in Los Angeles, a man beats the crooked roulette wheel. He places a large bet on number thirteen, which comes up. He lets it ride for a second time and wins again, then stakes the lot on thirteen again — and calmly walks out with a million dollars of winnings! When Sharky hires Johnny Merak to find the man who's taken his money, there's a spate of murders — with Johnny himself a candidate for death . . .

Books by John Glasby
in the Linford Mystery Library:

THE SAVAGE CITY
A TIME FOR MURDER
DEATH NEVER STRIKES TWICE
THE DARK DESTROYER
DARK CONFLICT
THE UNDEAD
DEATH COMES CALLING
MURDER IS MY SHADOW
DARK LEGION

JOHN GLASBY

THE WHEEL SPINS THIRTEEN

Complete and Unabridged

LINFORD
Leicester

First published in Great Britain

First Linford Edition
published 2009

British Library CIP Data

Glasby, John S. (John Stephen)
    The wheel spins thirteen - -
    (Linford mystery library)
    1. Gamblers- -California- -Los Angeles- -
    Fiction. 2. Suspense fiction.
    3. Large type books
    I. Title II. Series
    823.9'14–dc22

ISBN 978–1–84782–871–2

Published by
F. A. Thorpe (Publishing)
Anstey, Leicestershire

Set by Words & Graphics Ltd.
Anstey, Leicestershire
Printed and bound in Great Britain by
T. J. International Ltd., Padstow, Cornwall

This book is printed on acid-free paper

1

Strange Coincidence

It was an evening in late September when it all began. Sunset Strip was its usual gaudy self. Brilliant neon lights of every conceivable colour lined the sidewalks. Most of them had haloes around them where the mist was beginning to drift in from the ocean.

But even with the haloes there was nothing holy about these lights. They were there for only one reason. To tempt the passers-by into the casinos where they would soon be parted from their money.

I was simply walking along, minding my own business, when I suddenly found myself outside one of the largest of the casinos. Dawn Grahame, my partner in the P.I. business, had driven to Minneapolis for a few days to attend to her ill mother. Not that there was anything really wrong with the old girl. I reckoned she just wanted to make sure that I was being a gentleman and still treating her daughter like a lady.

Being at a loose end, I turned off the sidewalk and walked into the place. Why I acted on the impulse I couldn't say. Perhaps there is a destiny that shapes our ends. Maybe someone up there, or in my case more likely down below, had taken me by the scruff of the neck and thrust me inside.

The joint was no different from dozens of others along the Strip. Roulette tables, Faro, dice, poker — whatever you wanted to play, you'd find it there.

Even at that early hour of the evening, the place was crowded. If you knew what to look for, you could tell the professional gamblers from those who just went in for a laugh and an hour of entertainment.

The former simply sat there like statues, only their eyes and hands moving. Their faces never altered. They could have been carved on Mount Rushmore for all the change of expression you'd find on them. The latter were guys and dolls who moved around the various games hoping to make a big win. The truth is that the number of people who walked out of there with the jackpot you could count on your right hand with four fingers missing.

I walked over to the cashier and changed a twenty spot into chips. I wasn't feeling particularly lucky but I figured — what the hell? — twenty bucks wouldn't break the bank. There was a vacant seat at a table where they were playing twenty-one. I sat down. The dealer was a tall, statuesque blonde. She never smiled but she dealt the cards like a professional. Her dress left very little to the imagination. But I guess that if someone lost all they had, at least there was something to look at.

I drew a queen and a two. Calling for another card she dealt me the eight of spades. It was a good hand so I stuck with it. Then she turned over the ace of clubs and king of diamonds and I watched my chips disappear somewhere under the table.

After two more losing hands I decided I'd had enough. Clearly this wasn't my night. I made to get up, only to find two hands as big as shovels on my shoulders. It would have been easier to escape from Alcatraz than to get out of that grip.

Looking up I saw the man who was leaning over me like the Rock of Gibraltar. It was Sharky Dexter, the casino owner. I knew him slightly from the old days when he was quite a big man in the Organization. He was still a big man, both in the Mobs and in size.

'It's not often we see you down here these days, Johnny,' he grated in a voice like the rumbling of an avalanche.

'Well you know how it is, Sharky,' I replied. 'I like to see how the other half lives. Makes a change from looking for errant husbands or wives.'

'Of course, Johnny, I understand. And how is business these days?'

'It could be better.'

Sharky suddenly bent until his face was close to mine. In a low whisper, he muttered, 'It's possible I may be able to put some business your way, Johnny. If you're interested, follow me.'

I didn't like doing business with guys

like Dexter. It nearly always landed me in trouble — big trouble. Then I thought: What the hell? I'd take the Devil's dough so long as it paid the rent.

He led the way to a door in the far wall. I got some funny looks from a few of the guys seated at the tables. Maybe they were wondering if I was ever going to come out again. Sharky opened the door and stood on one side to let me enter.

The room was empty. I'd somehow expected a couple of his hired gorillas to be there in case there was any trouble he couldn't handle. Motioning me to the chair in front of the large desk, he went to a small cabinet, took out a bottle, and poured a generous measure into two glasses.

Since Dexter wasn't known for wasting good liquor on folk he didn't have time for, I guessed that whatever he had on his mind was pretty important and he desperately needed my help.

He sank down in the chair opposite me and slid one of the glasses across the table. It glided over the smooth, polished surface, coming to a stop in front of me without spilling a drop.

'What's on your mind, Sharky?' I asked finally.

Something was worrying him but he seemed to be having difficulty spitting it out. Then he said harshly, 'Something happened here tonight, Johnny. Something that should never have happened.'

'Go on,' I said.

He stared at me over the rim of his glass as he downed half of the liquor in a single swallow. Grimacing, he said, 'It was a little after six. I was standing at the front near the entrance with one of the boys. Then this little guy walks into the place. I spot him at once because he wasn't like our usual clientele. He was scruffy, around sixty-five, with shabby clothes and white hair that was all over the place. I had him figured for a bum who'd just walked in off the street.'

'So?' I asked as he paused.

'I was about to have him tossed out onto the sidewalk but he walks over to the cashier, puts down this big wad of bills, and asks for them to be changed for chips. He then looks around and goes over to the roulette table near the door. There he puts the whole lot on number thirteen.'

'Obviously he isn't a superstitious guy.'

'Yeah. But it so happens that number thirteen came up.'

'I see. Then I guess he was just plain lucky,' I remarked.

'Lucky — hell! He gets his winnings and I hear him tell the croupier to leave it all on thirteen.' He paused. 'That's when I decide to take over the table myself.'

'Just to make sure there was nothing between him and the croupier?' I prompted as he still hesitated.

'That's right. But thirteen comes up again — not once but twice with all that dough riding on it every time. Then he picks up his chips, asks for cash and walks out of here with more than a million dollars of my money.'

I shook my head. 'Sharky, that's absolutely impossible.'

I knew that, mathematically, it could happen that a number came up three, or more, times in succession. But that only happened if everything was left strictly to chance. Here, in the casino, nothing was left to chance. I knew, from the old days, how these tables operated.

There was a magnet under the table. If any punter looked to be winning a substantial amount, the croupier had only to press a small button and the magnet made sure that the ball fell on whichever number he wanted. It was, perhaps, possible to beat the mathematics — but no one could beat the tables.

Dexter slammed his fist down on the table. 'I know it's damned impossible!' He almost shouted the words. 'But I saw it happen.'

'Have you checked that everything was operating correctly?' I asked. 'Can you be sure of that croupier, that he didn't somehow fix things when the first bet was made?'

'I've checked every damned thing. Believe me, there's nothing to explain it.'

I couldn't imagine why he was telling me all of this. Somehow it had happened and that was all there was to it. 'So what do you want me to do?'

'I want you to find this guy, discover how this was done.'

'I see. And of course you want your dough back?'

'Too damned right I do. Nobody takes Sharky Dexter for a mug and leaves with all those bucks.'

Controlling his temper with an effort, he got up and went across to a safe set in the wall behind his desk. Putting in the combination, he spun the wheel and opened it, taking out a wad of notes. Counting some off, he replaced the rest and then came back to the table. 'There's five grand here. You'll get another five when this case is finished to my satisfaction.'

'Hell, Sharky, do you know what you're asking? There could be thousands of guys in L.A. who fit the description you've just given me.'

'Then it's up to you to find the needle in the haystack.' The tone of his voice implied that it would be very unwise for me to refuse. It was something I'd learned from past experience. The Big Men in the Organization could do a lot for you but they could also do things against you and the latter normally proved to be nasty.

I pushed the dollar bills into my wallet and got up. 'I'll let you know the minute I find out anything,' I told him.

His lips twitched into what was meant to be a smile but there was no mirth in it. 'Let me give you a piece of advice, Johnny.' he said. 'Keep those notes in your pocket, otherwise I can guarantee you won't have them by the end of the night.'

'You don't have to tell me that,' I answered. 'You forget, I know far too much about what goes on in places like this.'

I went out, feeling his eyes on me all the way to the door. Outside, it was now growing dark and more lights were coming on. The salt air was refreshing after the atmosphere inside the casino. As I walked slowly back to where I'd parked my car, I wondered whether I'd done the right thing in taking this case.

Maybe, as Dawn so often said, I should stick to finding erring husbands or wives. It was the kind of detective work I did best. It didn't pay much but it kept my head above water and in one piece.

I reached my apartment twenty minutes later and let myself in. After putting on the electric fire, I made myself a drink and went over everything Dexter had told me. None of it made any sense. Either that guy was some kind of magician — or he had a way of seeing into the future. Either way, it should never have happened.

But it had and it was up to me to find out how. Finishing my drink, I thought about having another but then decided against it. Whiskey wasn't the key to this problem — not even a good bourbon. I told myself that maybe I'd be able to see things a little more clearly in the morning.

But everything still seemed the same the next morning. The sun was shining, Dawn would be back in a couple of days, but I was still as confused as I'd been the night before.

Once in the office, I put on the electric kettle and made myself a strong black coffee. As Dawn wasn't there I poured in a slug of whiskey without feeling guilty. I was just sipping it slowly, when the phone rang.

My first guess was that it was Dexter ringing to check that I was still on the case. But it wasn't. A voice that I didn't know said, 'Mister Merak? Johnny Merak?' There was a definite accent to the voice but it was one I didn't recognize.

'That's my name,' I replied.

'I understand that you're a private detective. Is that correct?'

'It is,' I acknowledged.

'I have to see you urgently. This is vitally important.'

'I'm in my office right now. If you'd care to drop by, I — '

'No. Not at your office.'

'Then where shall I meet you?'

There was a pause, then, 'You're acquainted with the park near the city centre, I presume.'

'Sure. I know it.'

'Good. Then I'll meet you there in half an hour.'

'And how will I know you?'

There was a sound like a dry chuckle on the other end of the line. 'You don't know me, Mister Merak, but I know you.'

The line went dead. I sat staring down at the receiver for a few moments before replacing it. While I finished my coffee I tried to recall if I had ever heard that voice before. But nothing came to mind. Those little mice inside my head were beginning to stir.

Pushing my hat onto my head, I checked the .38 and then put it back into the shoulder holster. There had been something about that phone call that I didn't like. I'd known a lot of guys in the past and not all of them could be counted as friends. Some of them would still like to see me at the bottom of the sea staring up at the fishes.

Twenty minutes later I passed through the gates of the park and found myself a vacant bench near the edge of the lake. There were a lot of people around and I studied them closely to see if there was a face among them I remembered from the past. None of them, however, jogged any memory in my mind.

Then a voice said, 'I'm glad you came, Mister Merak, and on time too.'

13

I turned quickly. The little guy who stood a couple of feet away was in his late sixties with white hair and a lined, wrinkled face. He was a complete stranger, someone I was sure I'd never met before. He had a newspaper folded under one arm. Without another word he sat down on the bench beside me.

'All right.' I said. 'What is this all about? You obviously know me but I'm sure I've never seen you before.' There was a little finger of ice brushing up and down my spine but I tried to ignore it.

'My name is Sergei Karmov. As to how I know you . . . That goes back a long time to the days when you, like me, were in the Organization. I knew a lot about you in those days but since I was always in the background, I guess you never noticed me.'

'So how can I help you?'

'I don't want help for myself but for my brother, Igor.' He pulled out the newspaper and handed it to me, indicating an article on one of the centre pages. I didn't need to read the column, the headline told it all.

MYSTERY MAN TAKES SHARKY DEXTER FOR OVER A MILLION DOLLARS

I offered him back the paper but he indicated I was to keep it. Folding it carefully, I said, 'So it was your brother who took Dexter for all that dough.'

He nodded. 'I suppose you know all about it by now.'

'I was in that casino last night just after it happened,' I told him. 'And I should tell you that Dexter has already given me a retainer of five grand to find whoever did it. He's really mad and he wants his money back.'

'Somehow, I figured he might, which is why my brother is in big trouble.'

'Then I'm afraid I can't help you — or your brother. A conflict of interests you know.'

He pursed his lips into a tight line. 'Neither of us will tell anyone if you don't.' There was a note of pleading in his voice now.

'That isn't the point. I'm not worried about you or your brother. But I am worried about what Dexter will do to me

15

if he should find out I'm helping you. And there's always the chance I'll have my licence revoked.'

'I understand that. But whatever Dexter has paid you, I'll double.' There was desperation in his voice now and I was beginning to feel sorry for him.

'What you obviously don't understand is that if I were to do that, my own life could be over before I found any answers. Dexter is not the kind of man you cross and get away with it. There would be half a dozen hoodlums hunting me down within an hour.'

He sat looking as miserable as a dog that had forgotten where it had buried its bone. Finally, he said throatily, 'All I want you to do is keep a close watch on my brother. He's absolutely convinced that he's being followed and sooner or later they're going to kill him.'

I turned his proposition over in my mind. Inwardly, I was sure there was no one tailing his brother. If Dexter had discovered his identity, where he lived, and had put a tail on him until he decided what to do with him, then why had he just given me five thousand dollars? It didn't make sense. A more likely explanation was that the brother was unduly paranoid and imagining he was being followed.

'O.K.,' I said finally, 'I'll tell you what I'll do. I'll stake out his place for a few days and if he goes out, I won't be far behind. But I'll need a recent photograph of him and his address.'

He looked worried at that and there was a hint of suspicion in his eyes. 'If I do that, how do I know you won't turn him over to Dexter and collect your five thousand dollars?'

'You don't. You'll just have to trust me. You say you knew me in the old days. If you did, you'll know that once I give my word, I keep it.'

He turned that over in his mind for a while and then nodded. 'I guess I've no other choice.' He took out his wallet and brought out a small photograph. It had obviously been taken by one of the countless machines scattered around the city. The resemblance to the man who sat beside me was immediately obvious.

He looked about a couple of years younger and his hair was a little darker. I had the feeling that he was a man who thought a lot, possibly a teacher. While I studied it closely, my companion scribbled an address on a piece of paper. Handing it to me, he said, 'He doesn't know I've come to see you. I think he would be angry if he did.'

In response to the look of mute inquiry on my face he went on, 'It goes back to the old days in Russia. Then my family was followed everywhere by the secret police. That is why we had to get out and come to America.'

'I understand. Very well, Mister Karmov. I'll see what I can do to keep your brother safe. If I need to get in touch with you, how — ?'

'I'll be in touch with you,' he interrupted quickly. By way of explanation, he added, 'You see, unlike you, I'm still in the Organization.'

I left him sitting on the bench, staring at nothing in particular and walked back to my car. I didn't like the position I'd got myself into. I could make another five grand by simply going to Sharky and spilling everything I knew about Karmov but that would be tantamount to killing the little old guy myself.

His blood would be on my hands and that wasn't something that appealed to me. Or if I managed to keep everything concealed from Dexter long enough for Karmov to figure out what he intended to do with all that dough, I might just get away with saving my own skin. I slid behind the wheel of the Merc and looked down at the piece of paper Sergei had given me. It was an address in the Hollywood area.

Glancing at my watch I saw it wanted a quarter to eleven. Time enough to get out there and look the place over. Besides, deep down inside, I had the feeling there was something here that didn't quite add up. Sergei had seemed too eager to tell me about his brother even though he must have known there was a strong possibility I'd turn Igor over to Dexter and collect that other five grand.

Those little mice inside my head were scampering around now, warning me that this could be a well-thought out plan to get me off this case permanently. Sergei had admitted he still worked for the Mob. If he'd had his ear tuned to the grapevine he'd know that Dexter had hired me to track down his brother.

It might have been a coincidence that he had phoned me the very next day after Sharky had hired me. The trouble was, I didn't believe in coincidences — just cause and effect.

After consulting my road map, I drove out to the place where Igor Markov was presumably hiding from the Organization, checking the house numbers as I drove slowly past.

This wasn't the fancy part of Hollywood where most of the stars, movie directors, and producers lived. The houses were dismal like little old ladies knitting away while their final years slipped past them, unnoticed. I parked the car a short distance from the house where Sergei's brother reputedly lived. It looked no different from the rest except that, if Sergei had told me the truth, there was a little guy in there with over a million dollars of Organization dough.

I opened the newspaper Sergei had given me and pretended to read it while keeping the house on the opposite side of the street under close observation. The curtains were drawn across all of the windows and outwardly there seemed to be no signs of life.

Then I saw one of the downstairs curtains twitch slightly. It might have been the wind but more likely someone inside was keeping me under observation. If Igor was in there he had obviously spotted my car and was doubtless wondering just who was sitting behind the wheel. I sat there for another ten minutes but nothing more happened.

I was on the point of turning the key in the ignition when the front door suddenly opened and these two guys came out. Both were over six feet tall and certainly didn't fit the picture I'd been given of Igor Karmov. I settled myself further back in my seat.

Either these punks had been hired by Igor to provide him with some protection — or they were Dexter's boys. If they

21

were the latter it was possible that Karmov was lying somewhere in that house with a bullet in him.

I studied the two guys closely as they stood on the top step talking in low voices. They seemed edgy, nervous. One kept glancing along the street in both directions, his right hand in his pocket. He looked over in my direction and muttered something to his companion.

For a moment I thought he meant to walk over and ask me what I was doing just sitting there but a few seconds later, a black limousine appeared around the far corner. It drew up smoothly by the sidewalk in front of the house and both guys got in. The car moved off with a roar as the driver put his foot down hard.

I waited until it had disappeared around the corner at the intersection, then got out and walked over to Karmov's house. The front door was still open. That fact started alarm bells ringing inside my head, loud enough to waken those little mice. Now they were telling me that I should get out of there fast and tell any suspicions I had to the cops.

But I'd taken the case and I meant to stick with it. Stepping into the hallway with its oak-panelled walls, I called Karmov's name. I didn't expect any answer and I didn't get one. The whole place seemed as quiet as the grave. But there was something not quite right — I could feel it in my bones.

Taking out my .38, I opened the door on my left. It was the room where I'd seen the curtains twitch but there was no one there. Everything seemed to be in order. It was the same on the whole of the ground floor. Nothing had been disturbed in any way. Very slowly I made my way up the creaking stairs. The first bedroom I came to was also empty but the second —

There was a guy lying on the bed near the wide window. I knew then why there had been no answer to my call. This guy was obviously not Igor Karmov — and he was clearly unable to answer anyone. There was a dark red stain on his white shirt and it would have been clear even to someone with a white stick that he hadn't been dead for very long.

He looked to be in his mid-thirties, well

dressed, black hair parted in the middle. Somehow, his face seemed familiar but I couldn't put a name to it. Straightening up I made for the door but before I could reach it there was the sound of heavy footsteps pounding up the stairs and a moment later, three guys burst in.

One of them was just an ordinary patrolman. The other two were Lieutenant O'Leary and Sergeant Kolowinski of the LAPD. O'Leary threw a quick glance towards the stiff on the bed and then looked round at me. His expression was far from pleasant.

'Merak,' he said thinly. 'Why is it that whenever there's a crime you're to be found on the scene?'

'I guess it's just one of those unfortunate hands that fate seems to deal me, Lieutenant,' I replied. 'And if you're thinking that I shot this guy, you'd better think again. Judging by the appearance of that chest wound, I'd guess he was shot with a small caliber bullet — maybe a .22. And my gun — ' I handed it to him. ' — is a .38 and you can see for yourself that it hasn't been fired.'

He took the weapon and sniffed the barrel, then gave it back. 'All right, Merak. So you didn't kill him.' He looked disappointed. 'Do you know who he is?'

I shook my head. 'He looks vaguely familiar but I can't put a name to him.'

'He can't have been dead for more than half an hour, Lieutenant,' Kolowinski said. 'That bullet wound is still bleeding.'

O'Leary's eyebrows went up so far they almost vanished under his hat. 'So what the hell are you doing here, Merak? And don't tell me you just came along for a stroll.'

I ignored the sarcasm. 'I came to see the guy who lives here,' I told him. 'I figured he might be in some kind of danger.'

'Evidently he was.' O'Leary inclined his head towards the body.

'That stiff isn't the owner of this place. From the information I've been given the guy who lives here is named Igor Karmov. Here's a picture of him.' I handed him the photograph Sergei had given me. 'Even you can see there's not the slightest resemblance.'

He studied the picture for a moment and then gave a reluctant nod. 'So we're left with a stiff with no name and a missing Igor Karmov.' he grunted finally. He turned to Kolowinski. 'It seems we have a mystery here, Sergeant.'

'There's one other thing I think you should know, Lieutenant,' I said.

'Oh, what's that?'

'I was parked just across the street keeping an eye on this place. Two guys came out and left in a black limousine. That was when I decided to come in and take a look around.'

'So you reckon they could be the killers?'

'It seems a logical conclusion.'

'All right. Give the Sergeant a description of these two guys. Not that there's much chance of tracing them if they're professional hitmen. I don't suppose you got the licence number of the car?'

I shook my head. 'They took off too fast for me to get it.'

'Too bad.' He swung on the patrolman standing quietly just inside the door. 'Put out an APB on this guy.' He handed him the photograph of Igor Karmov, then turned to me. 'All right, Merak. You can go. But don't take any unexpected vacations out of town. I'll want to question you again.'

'I'd like that photograph back when you've finished with it, Lieutenant.'

'You'll get it in the morning.'

I went out, back to my car. I had a lot to think about. This case had suddenly developed a whole new set of angles, some of which didn't make any sense. If Sergei had told the truth, where the hell was his brother? Had that dead guy been one of Dexter's boys who had somehow tracked Karmov down and the latter had shot him when he asked for the money? And who were those two guys who'd left the house, obviously just after the murder?

I was beginning to wish that Dawn were back to give me the benefit of some of her feminine intuition. At the moment I was stuck with more questions than there were answers.

Heading back to the office, I'd just unlocked the door when the phone started ringing. It was an impatient kind of ring, not the melodious sort when a new client came on asking for help. Picking it up, I sank into my chair and said, 'Merak.'

It was Sharky Dexter's dulcet tones. 'I've just heard that you've been found with some stiff out Hollywood way — also that the police are involved. What the hell's going on, Merak?'

'This is nothing to do with your case, Sharky,' I said smoothly. 'I was just tying up some loose ends from an old job I had to finish.'

'Then make damned sure my name doesn't come into it. I don't like it when the cops start probing into my business.'

I can imagine. I spoke the words to myself. There was no point in antagonizing him. At least, not until I got my other five grand.

'One thing I have to ask, Sharky,' I said. 'You haven't sent any of your boys out looking for this guy who took you for all that dough?'

'No.' He sounded indignant. 'That's a funny kind of question to ask. Why should

I do that when I've paid you good money to do it for me?'

'I just had to ask. I got the feeling that somebody else is interested in this guy.'

'Well, it's nothing to do with me. I reckon you'd better find out who these other people are and make sure they don't foul things up.'

'I'll do that,' I replied and put the phone down. Sitting back, I contemplated my next move. At the moment, there didn't seem much I could do. O'Leary would have that house cordoned off as a crime scene so there was no chance of getting in there and nosing around.

I got to my feet and went over to put the kettle on and make myself a coffee. I'd just switched it on when the door opened. Without turning, I said sharply, 'Don't you usually knock?'

'Now that isn't the way to greet a lady,' said a familiar voice, 'particularly when she's been away for a few days.'

I swung round. Dawn stood there looking as beautiful as ever. Somehow, I found my voice. 'Am I glad to see you,' I said. 'I didn't expect you back for another couple of days. How's your mother?'

'She's fine now. She always makes out everything is far worse than it really is.'

She walked up to me. 'I've missed you too, Johnny. Now don't just stand there. Kiss me.'

I did. When we finally broke apart, she went on, 'Now finish making that coffee and tell me everything that's been happening while I've been away. Are you working on another case?'

I waited until we were seated and drinking the hot coffee before answering her question. As briefly as possible I went over all that had happened since that brief time I had spent in the casino. By the time I'd finished her brow was furrowed in concentration. She sat quite still, biting her lower lip. Finally, she said, 'So you're back working with one of the Mob.'

'As far as that's concerned, I'm merely trying to find the guy who fleeced Dexter and get his money back for him,' I said lamely. It was a poor excuse and I knew she didn't like the idea one little bit.

'So what are you going to do now, taking into account that you're back in

O'Leary's bad books?'

'O'Leary knows he's got nothing on me. The two things that worry me at the moment are — where is Igor Karmov now and who's this stiff I found in his house?'

I finished my coffee and set the cup down on the table. 'I reckon the next step is to try and find out something about the Karmov brothers. They're undoubtedly at the bottom of all this.'

'I'll see what I can dig up.'

'But it's your first day back,' I protested.

'Then it's about time I did some work. To be honest, you just seem to be floundering around in the dark.'

I knew it was useless to argue with her. Once she'd made up her mind to do something nothing short of a direct order from the President would stop her.

She left five minutes later taking her notebook with her. Less than a minute after she had gone the phone rang again. This time it was Lieutenant O'Leary.

'I thought I'd let you know that we've identified the dead guy we found. Seems he's a small-time crook, named Jervis. He was pulled in for involvement in the murder of Marco Torrenco one of the gang bosses, but there was insufficient evidence and he got off with only two years for carrying an unlicensed weapon.'

'And where is this top guy now?' I asked.

'If you're thinking he might be responsible, I'm afraid you're wrong. He got fifteen years and he's still in the state penitentiary.'

I uttered a short laugh. 'You know better than that, Lieutenant. Even from a prison cell these hoods can arrange a killing on the outside just by snapping their fingers.'

'I'm well aware of that, Merak,' he replied sharply. 'And I hope you're not mixed up with this case. This is now a police matter and I want you to stay out of it. You're already a suspect.' With that, he slammed down the phone.

I knew he meant every word. He was that type of cop — played it all by the book and as straight as they came. He only had one fault. He didn't like private detectives who poked their noses into what he considered was his business.

It was almost an hour later when Dawn arrived back. Lighting a cigarette, I leaned back in my chair and said, 'Well, did you find anything?'

'A little.' She sat down and opened her notebook, glancing through the pages. 'I must confess there's something odd about the Karmov brothers.'

'Odd in what way?' I asked.

'I've managed to discover quite a lot about Sergei Karmov. It seems he's one of Malloy's men and he has a police record as long as your arm, including bringing in weapons from Eastern Europe and drug dealing. On the last offence he cut a deal with the D.A. Gave the name and whereabouts of the Mister Big and got off with a reduced sentence.'

'He seems to be quite a busy little guy. It's strange I never came across him in the old days. And Igor?'

'That's the really odd bit.' She looked puzzled. 'I couldn't find a single thing about him. It's almost as if he doesn't exist.'

'That is strange,' I agreed. Those little mice inside my head had woken up at that point. This was the last thing I'd expected and they were telling me that, for some reason, Sergei was lying and had made up this mysterious brother to cover up the fact that he was the one who had taken Dexter for all that dough.

So either he was playing a very clever game using me as the patsy — or he did have an older brother who had somehow disappeared. Whichever it was, I figured I should have another talk with Sergei — and that wasn't going to be easy.

I had no idea where he lived and no phone number. Until he took it into his head to contact me again I was stymied.

2

Murder lends a hand

It was two days later when the phone rang with Sergei on the other end of the line. He sounded strange, agitated. 'Are you alone, Merak?' he asked.

I looked around the office. Not even the invisible man was there, so I said, 'Yes, I'm alone. What's on your mind?'

'This is Sergei Karmov. I have to see you right away. It's urgent. I want you to meet me now. Please don't interrupt. I'll be waiting at the place where we last met. It might be dangerous if I were to meet you at your office.' The phone went dead.

I sat for a moment staring at the receiver in my hand. There was something wrong here. All of the words had come out in a rush and Sergei had sounded as though he was in the kind of trouble only the Organization could dish out.

I scribbled a note to Dawn telling her

what had happened and left it on her desk. I could have voiced my suspicions to Lieutenant O'Leary but I figured he'd not take the slightest notice. At the moment I was way down his list of people he'd send Christmas cards to.

I drove out to the park. Here I made my way to the seat by the lake where I'd first met the old guy. I expected to see him sitting there, waiting for me to show up. But he wasn't. There was a couple of kids kicking a ball around on the grass and a few folk strolling around — but no sign of Sergei.

I sat down and waited, figuring that perhaps he'd been held up on the way. As the minutes passed, however, it occurred to me that perhaps something more sinister had delayed him. Maybe it was just my naturally suspicious mind but those little mice inside my head were telling me that Sergei had sounded really desperate on the phone and that whatever was keeping him had nothing to do with the early morning traffic.

After a while, I decided that, whatever had happened, he wasn't going to show. I got up and at that moment, one of the kids uttered a sudden shout. He was pointing towards the lake.

I turned quickly to look in the direction of his pointing finger. There was something near the middle of the water and even from that distance it looked like a body. As I stood there wondering what to do, a big guy suddenly threw off his jacket, kicked off his shoes, and dived in.

Somehow, he got him and a few moments later had dragged the body to the side. A crowd gathered like flies around a pot of jam. I pushed my way through them and looked down, recognizing the dead man at once. It was Sergei Karmov.

A woman screamed hysterically. Then someone else yelled, 'Somebody call the cops and a doctor.'

A couple of guys ran off towards the gate. I went down on one knee beside the body. Knowing that everyone was watching me, I went through Sergei's pockets. There was nothing; not even a parking ticket. It was then I also noticed the blood on the side of his head and another wider red stain on the front of his shirt.

'Has he been drowned?' queried the guy next to me.

I shook my head. 'He's been shot through the heart,' I told him. The hysterical dame began screaming again. 'I'd say he was murdered some place away from here and then his body dumped into the middle of the lake.'

I pushed myself to my feet and a few moments later a too-familiar voice shouted, 'Get everybody away from there, Sergeant.'

Lieutenant O'Leary came striding towards me. He saw me almost at once and his features assumed a blend of incredulous disbelief and irritation. 'You again, Merak!' His voice sounded like a saw rasping on metal. 'Sometimes I get the feeling you commit these murders yourself just to annoy me.'

'I reckon you'd really like to pin them on me, Lieutenant.'

'That thought has occurred to me on a number of occasions,' he muttered sarcastically. He went down beside the body. 'What happened here?'

When no one spoke, I said, 'One of the

kids playing here spotted him in the middle of the lake and someone went in and pulled him out.'

As the onlookers crowded forward to get a better view, O'Leary yelled, 'I told you to get all of these people away from this area, Sergeant. Do it!'

Kolowinski came forward and began herding them away.

'Not you, Merak,' he snapped as I edged back from the body. 'I want to talk to you. Clearly he wasn't shot here. Whoever tried to hide the body in the lake obviously made a mess of the job. But there are no documents on him. Absolutely nothing at all.'

He turned to the folk gathered around. 'Any of you know who he is?'

When no one answered, I said, 'His name's Sergei Karmov, Lieutenant.'

O'Leary turned back to me.

There was a nasty look in his eyes as he said, 'So you know him, Merak. Now, why didn't I guess that right away?'

'He's a client of mine, or at least he was. He telephoned me less than an hour ago to come here and meet him. He said he had something extremely urgent to tell me.'

'So why here? Why not at your office?'

'He thought it would be dangerous to meet there.'

'Dangerous for whom? You — or him?'

'I've no idea, Lieutenant. He didn't say.'

He made as if to say something more but at that moment a tall guy carrying a case pushed through the crowd. I guessed he was the doctor.

He bent beside the body and examined it carefully before straightening up. 'There's very little water in his lungs that I can see so it appears fairly obvious he was dead before he was put into the lake. I'd say he sustained those abrasions on his head when he fell after being shot. Judging by the bullet wound my opinion is that he died instantly.'

'Any idea how long he's been dead, doctor?' O'Leary asked.

'I can't give you an accurate figure at the moment, that will have to wait for an autopsy. But my guess would be between six and eight hours.'

'But that's utterly impossible,' I protested. 'He was speaking to me on the phone about forty minutes ago.'

The doctor looked across at me. 'I can assure you, Mister — ?'

'Merak,' I said, 'I'm a private investigator.'

'Well, Mister Merak, I can assure you that whoever spoke to you on the phone, it was definitely not this man!'

I felt as if I'd just been hit over the head by a baseball bat. I couldn't doubt what the doctor had just said but those little mice were now screaming at me, telling me that this case was getting screwier by the minute.

O'Leary took me by the arm and led me away from the scene. Harshly, he said, 'I reckon you know a lot more about this murder than you're telling me, Merak. That stiff back there — is he the one you were telling me about.'

'Yes. He's the one with the brother I'm supposed to look out for.'

'The one who disappeared?'

'That's the one,' I affirmed.

O'Leary rubbed his chin. He looked as

puzzled as I felt. Then he muttered, half to himself, 'This doesn't make any kind of sense.' He threw a quick glance at the Sergeant. 'Take a look around and see if there's any sign of a vehicle having been used recently in the park. I somehow doubt if he was carried here from the place where he was shot.'

After a quick search of the place, Kolowinski came back, shaking his head. 'Nothing there, Lieutenant. But they tell me they have a motorized trailer they often use for carrying gardening equipment and taking away dead branches.'

I waited to see if he was going to ask any more questions but when he remained silent, staring back at the body, I said, 'Do you need me any more, Lieutenant?'

He considered that; then shook his head. 'You can go for the time being, Merak. But I'll want to talk to you again once we've finished here.'

'Thanks, Lieutenant. You know where to find me.'

'Just get the hell out of here and let me do my job.'

I left. At the gate, a couple of

uniformed officers stopped me. When I showed my business card and told them O'Leary had finished questioning me, they reluctantly let me pass.

I got back to the office fifteen minutes later and found that Dawn had arrived while I'd been away. She gave me an inquiring look but said nothing until I'd seated myself behind the desk.

'More trouble, Johnny?' she said after a brief pause.

'Afraid so. Big trouble. That client, Sergei Karmov, rang me just as soon as I got in.'

'Oh.' She busied herself making coffee. 'What did he want this time?'

'He asked me to meet him by the lake in the park. He sounded really agitated so I went right away. Only he didn't show up. Not alive anyway. He was floating in the middle of the lake. They got him out but he'd been shot before being tossed into the water. The doctor is adamant he'd been dead between five and six hours.'

Her delicately curved eyebrows went up an inch. 'But he phoned you less than an hour ago.'

'I know . . . '

'Then how — ?'

'How could he speak to me on the phone when he was already dead? I don't know. The only thing I can come up with was that it was someone else who phoned me. Or perhaps — ' I paused as another thought struck me. 'Or perhaps that wasn't Sergei but a recording he'd been forced to make just before he was killed.'

'Then that must have been the killer who rang you and for some reason he wanted you to be in the park when they found him. But that still doesn't answer why?'

'Unless whoever it was figured I might be getting a little too close to the truth and wanted to pin the killing on me.'

She put the coffee down in front of me and placed her hands on my shoulders. 'If you want my opinion, Johnny, you're getting into this too deep for your own safety. If this client is dead, you don't owe him anything. Get out of it while you can.'

I knew she was making sense. Sergei had told me that he was still working for the Organization. If they were behind his murder and I persisted in probing any further, I could find myself in deep trouble.

But there were now too many loose ends hanging around and they were the kind you could trip over if you weren't careful. I finished my coffee. Dawn was watching me apprehensively.

'Somehow,' I said, 'I doubt if Lieutenant O'Leary will let me drop the case as easily as that. He clearly has a niggling impression that I'm more involved in Sergei's murder than I really am.'

'Has he any reason for such an absurd idea?' she demanded.

'Two reasons. Firstly he knows I was working for Sergei and secondly, he's the kind of cop who believes the primary suspect is the one who's around when the body is discovered.'

'That's ridiculous.'

'Try telling that to him.' The words were barely out of my mouth when there came a loud knock on the door and it was opened to reveal O'Leary with Kolowinski close behind him.

45

'Do come in, Lieutenant,' I said pointedly.

He ignored the sarcasm and lowered himself into the chair opposite. 'You know why I'm here,' he said harshly. 'I want to go over your statement again. There are still some points that don't add up. Not to my satisfaction, anyway.'

'I figured that might be the case.'

'I understand you were working for the victim. May I ask what you were doing for him?'

'You can ask, Lieutenant, but there's still such a thing as client confidentiality and — '

'Don't give me that hogwash.' His broad features turned even redder than usual. 'This is a murder inquiry, Merak, and I don't give a damn about any confidentiality. Besides, your client is dead now. If there's anything I should know, you'll tell me now — or you can come down to the station if you prefer.'

'Somehow, I get the feeling you'd like to pin this murder on me,' I said.

'It's crossed my mind.'

'The trouble with that idea is that I'm not in the habit of bumping off my clients. I'd soon go out of business if I did that. Just think of the dough I'd lose.'

'All right. Don't try to be funny with me. What do you know about this guy, Sergei Karmov? Who was he working for?'

'He told me he still worked in the Organization but he didn't enlarge on that. Just that he might find himself in trouble if they should find out he'd asked me for help.'

O'Leary pulled his chair a little closer to the desk. 'And what help was that?'

'It seems his brother is in big trouble. I don't know if you read about it in the papers but his brother, Igor, was the guy who took Sharky Dexter for over a million dollars on the roulette table, betting on the number thirteen to come up three times in succession.'

The Lieutenant whistled thinly through his teeth.

'I read about it, Lieutenant,' Kolowinski put in. 'Seems Dexter was pretty sore about it.'

O'Leary smiled. I reckon it was the first time that had happened. He should have taken a photograph of it and had it framed. 'I can imagine. And no doubt Dexter wants his money back.'

I didn't mention a word about Dexter hiring me to trace Karmov. I figured the less he knew about that little deal, the better.

'Do you have any idea where this Igor Karmov might be now?'

I shook my head. 'None at all, Lieutenant. For all I know he's skipped the country and is now enjoying a life in the sunshine down in the Caribbean. At least that's what I'd do if I had all that dough.'

O'Leary considered that for a little while and then heaved himself heavily to his feet. 'Knowing you, Merak, I think you're considering trying to locate this guy. If you are — and you do manage to find him — you'll tell me first. There are some questions I want to ask him about a first degree murder.'

'You reckon he killed his own brother?'

'No. But I'm as sure as hell that he killed that guy we found on Wiltshire.'

He went out, trailing Sergeant Kolowinski behind him like a dog on a leash. I watched them go. There were lots of thoughts swirling around in my mind but few of them made any sense.

Of one thing I was certain. Karmov hadn't killed that punk on Wiltshire Boulevard as O'Leary believed. Having said that, however, there was a whole lot I didn't know about this little guy and that was something I intended to remedy right away.

Grabbing my hat, I made for the door. Dawn turned and looked at me in surprise. 'You going somewhere, Johnny?'

I paused. 'You couldn't find anything about Igor Karmov. I think it's time we probed a little deeper and I reckon I know where I can get that information.'

'Be careful, Johnny. If they could get to Sergei, they can get to you.'

'I'll watch my back,' I promised. I'd already decided on the first person I wanted to see. Sharky Dexter. I knew that if I didn't contact him soon he'd come looking for me and that was something I didn't want to happen. Dexter was not a patient man. He wanted things doing immediately. Not that I had much to tell him but this time I figured he might be able to help me.

The casino was open when I got there and well patronized even at that hour. There was no sign of Sharky when I went in but a couple of his bruisers must have recognized me from my last visit for they immediately drifted in my direction.

'You got any information for the boss?' asked one of them. His tone implied that if I hadn't I better leave and start walking.

'Some,' I replied. 'Now do I get to see him or not?'

'This way.' One of them took my arm and led me towards the far door. Knocking, he opened it and said, 'Someone to see you, boss.'

Dexter glanced up from behind the desk. 'Johnny! I was debating whether I might have to send a couple of my boys to look for you. It seems so long since we last met.'

'Less than a week, Sharky,' I said as the door closed softly behind me. 'These things take time.'

'Of course, of course. And what have you got for me? Good news, I hope.'

I sat down in the other chair. 'Some news,' I told him. 'I can give you the name of the guy who took your million dollars. His name is Igor Karmov.'

I watched his face closely as I gave the name, watching for any sign of recognition. But there was nothing. He shook his head slowly. 'The name means nothing to me,' he said finally.

'Then how about Sergei Karmov?'

He stiffened at that. Going around the desk, he sat down, his fingers gripping the edge of the desk, his knuckles standing out white beneath the skin.

'Evidently that name means quite a lot to you,' I remarked.

Through his teeth, Dexter muttered, 'He works for Malloy now but years ago, he was one of the top men with Carlos Galecci. The cops got him for bringing in cocaine from South America. He should have done twenty years but he only got five by making a deal. He shopped my brother to the D.A. He died in prison after they sent him up for thirty years.'

'But you don't know anything about his brother?'

'Not a thing. But now you've given me his name I'll soon find him even if I have to get his whereabouts out of Sergei.'

'I'm afraid that won't be possible,' I told him.

He glared at me across the desk. 'Why not?'

'Sergei's dead. He was murdered this morning. I was there when they found his body in the park. He'd been shot and must have died instantly. It was clear, however, that he'd been murdered somewhere else and dumped there in the lake.'

That seemed to have momentarily caught him off balance. I decided to push him a little harder before he could digest all of the implications behind Sergei's killing. 'You have close connections with Joe Malloy and his outfit. If, as he told me, Sergei worked for Joe you might have heard something which may explain this murder.'

He sat up straight in his chair. He seemed to have regained a little of his composure for he snapped, 'Now why should I tell you that?'

'Because it may help me to find this

brother of his. At the moment no one seems to know a single thing about him. His brother is the only lead I have. Do you know if there was a hit out on Sergei and if so who ordered it. If there was, it might help me a lot.'

He narrowed down his eyes and his next question was one I never expected. 'How far in are you with Manzelli? From what I've heard you've done him a few favours in the past.'

'Enrico Manzelli!' He was the Big Boss, the man who ruled all of the various organizations in Los Angeles. Nothing happened without him knowing about it. He held the matter of life and death over everyone in the Mobs. 'Are you saying that he gave the order for Sergei Karmov to be eliminated?'

Dexter gave a jerky nod. 'That's my belief.'

I felt a little finger of ice brush along my spine. If what Dexter had just intimated was true I was certainly getting much deeper into this case than I liked. The fact that I'd been of help to Manzelli on a number of occasions in the past would count as nothing if he thought I was a menace to the smooth running of the Mobs.

I would go the same way as Sergei and there would be no questions asked. I would simply disappear into the ocean or be found in some alley with a slug in me. Johnny Merak would be history.

Across from me, Dexter seemed to have reached a sudden decision. He scraped back his chair and crossed to the safe in the far wall. Opening it, he took out some dollar bills, counted them out and tossed them onto the desk in front of me.

'Five grand,' he said thinly. 'That concludes our deal, Merak. You're no longer working for me.'

'But the deal was to find this guy and get you your dough back.'

'I'm changing the deal,' he rasped. 'Quite suddenly, you're getting too dangerous to know. Now take your money and get out. Don't try to come into any of my places for whatever reason. You won't be allowed through the door.'

He saw me out, onto the sidewalk. He

was still watching as I turned the corner. The mere fact that I had mentioned the connection between Sergei and Malloy seemed to have unnerved him.

I guess I should have done what he said and dropped this case like a hot potato but I'd been in tight spots before and I didn't like leaving cases half completed and murders without finding the killer. As I walked back to the Merc I turned over in my mind the other leads I had.

Jack Kolowinski was always good for information from the police side if I got him in the right mood. I was also on talking terms with both Sam Rizzio and Joe Malloy, the bosses of two of the biggest organizations. As I slid behind the wheel I checked my watch. It was almost two. Knowing his habits of old, I guessed that at that moment Malloy would be having lunch at his favourite restaurant — the Comero.

As I'd figured, he was in his usual seat at the far wall, facing the door, when I walked in twenty minutes later. Two of his minders were seated one on either side of him. I didn't approach him right away but found a table only a short distance away where he could see me clearly.

It didn't take him long to spot me. As always, his eyes were everywhere. A very nervous guy he made certain he recognized everyone there, particularly if there was anyone who disliked him sufficiently to do him some permanent damage.

'Johnny!' He yelled my name loudly to make sure I heard it above the general murmur of conversation. He motioned me to join him, pointing a stubby finger at the chair opposite him. 'Have a seat. We can't have an old friend eating alone.'

'Thanks Joe,' I said, sitting down.

'Think nothing of it. Besides, I've been meaning to call on you. I understand you've been talking with someone who works for me, Sergei Karmov.'

'I'm afraid he won't be working for you any more,' I said, watching his reaction.

'What's that supposed to mean?' His tone changed as his small, deep-set eyes bored into me like drills.

'He was found this morning with a slug in his chest. Someone had shot him and dumped his body in the lake in the park.'

He laid his knife and fork down neatly beside his plate. 'If this is some kind of joke, Merak, I'm not amused.'

'It's no joke, Joe. As a matter of fact I was there when his body was pulled out of the water.'

His face looked even more ugly than usual — if that were possible. He glanced sideways at his two companions. 'I think you'd better spill everything you know, Merak,' he snarled. I noticed he didn't call me Johnny now.

'There's not much I can tell you. I got a phone call from Sergei this morning asking me to meet him in the park. I got there within fifteen minutes but he didn't show up so I decided not to wait for him. Then a kid playing football spotted this body in the water. Some guy went in and got him out. Like I said, he'd been shot through the heart. The funny thing is that according to the evidence he'd been dead for more than two hours.'

'Yet you're saying he called you less than twenty minutes earlier.'

'The guy sounded just like Sergei. My bet is that the killer forced him to record that phone message before he was shot. Obviously it wasn't him unless he was calling from beyond the grave.'

Malloy pushed his plate away from him. Evidently he'd suddenly lost his appetite. Very slowly, he said, 'Karmov worked for me for almost fifteen years. He was a good man. Whoever killed him meant to hit me hard.'

'And to frame me for his murder,' I said.

'So where do you come into it?'

'He hired me to follow his brother, Igor. He figured that someone was out to kill him.'

Malloy leaned forward as far as his bulk would allow. 'You got any idea who was after his brother? If you do, you'd better tell me now. So far, you seem to have led a charmed life but if you cross me, that will come to an end very soon.'

I knew he meant every word. Malloy never made any threats he couldn't carry out.

'Sure — it was Sharky Dexter.'

'Dexter? He's the guy who runs that string of casinos on Sunset.' He looked again at the two gorillas flanking him at the table. 'It seems to me we should pay Dexter a little visit. He appears to be getting a little too big for his breeches.'

'Then you can't tell me anything at all about Sergei's brother, Igor?'

'Nothing at all, Merak. In fact, I never knew Sergei had a brother.'

So there I had it — just another blind alley with nothing at the end of it.

Outside the Comero, standing on the sidewalk, I lit a cigarette and watched the smoke drift away in lazy spirals. At that moment any ideas I had seemed as intangible as the smoke. From the moment I'd walked into Dexter's place I seemed to have opened a can of worms and right now they were wriggling all over the city.

At the heart of them all was a little white-haired man who had somehow beaten the system and found a way of taking Sharky for a million bucks. Everything came back to him. But L.A. is a big place and there are thousands of holes where a rat could hide. The Organization, with its tentacles stretching everywhere would get him in the end — but it might take a long time.

I flicked my cigarette butt away and turned to go back to my car only to find my way blocked by two guys each built like a mountain. One of them said quietly, 'I'm sure you don't want to make a scene, Merak. Just walk with us, nice and quietly, around the next corner.'

I did as I was told. A few folk on the sidewalk gave us funny looks and then hurried on. They knew what was happening. When guys like my two friends take you off the street nobody wants to interfere.

There was a large black limousine waiting just around the corner. With the exception of the windscreen all of the others were blacked out.

'You've got the wrong guy,' I said hoarsely.

The bruiser on my left uttered a laugh like the howl of a hyena. 'We never get the wrong guy,' he said. 'Now get inside.'

His companion had opened the rear door. I was thrust inside, falling into the back seat and bumping into an enormous bulk seated there. Jerking myself upright I turned to face the guy sitting beside me.

That was when I knew I was in really big trouble. I recognized him immediately. Enrico Manzelli!

The fact that he was sitting there and not tucked away in his mansion several miles out in the country told me that something really important was afoot. Manzelli had never been known to leave his isolated home among the hills apart from the time, several years back, when he had to face a grand jury.

I couldn't recall what the charge had been but his lawyer had got him off and since that time he'd remained shut away from the outside world. Leaning forward, he said something in a low voice to the guy behind the wheel. A moment later, we pulled away from the sidewalk and into the main flow of traffic.

Without looking at me he said, 'I'm very disappointed in you, Merak. I expect incompetence and stupidity from some of the men I control but I thought you had, at least, a small amount of sense.'

I shifted myself into a more comfortable

position. I wasn't sure what was coming next but I knew it wouldn't be nice. Somewhere along the line I'd evidently done something that Manzelli didn't like so I waited for him to tell me.

When he saw that I wasn't going to say anything, he went on evenly, 'As you know, my job is to see that everything in the city runs smoothly and without trouble. If anything should happen to upset that balance, I have to take steps to rectify it.

'You have, wittingly or unwittingly, upset that state of equilibrium. Dexter is angry because someone has outsmarted him. Malloy has lost one of his best men and is determined to find, and eliminate, whoever did it. I won't bore you with any more details except to say that such things are being exacerbated by one man — you.

'I think you can see that, in my position, Merak, I cannot allow this to continue. Something has to be done.'

His tone had become more and more menacing. I knew I was now in the tightest spot of my life. I'd seen what happened to anyone who fell foul of the Big Men in the Organization — and Manzelli was undoubtedly the biggest. If you didn't just permanently disappear, they had their henchmen beat you up so that you were just a crippled shell for the rest of your life. It wasn't a nice thought.

'So it was a mistake to take Karmov's case,' I said.

He pursed his thick lips before speaking, then said, 'I would say it was an error of judgment on your part. Your big mistake was accepting Dexter's money in return for finding the man who beat the roulette wheel.'

Glancing through what little I could see of the windscreen I noticed that we were heading out of town into open country — but this was not the way to Manzelli's palatial home. That made me even more nervous. I had the inescapable feeling that Manzelli intended to act rather than talk.

'How could I possibly have known at the time that all of this was going to happen?'

'Perhaps you may act more carefully the next time, if there is a next time.' He turned his head and stared straight at me. It was impossible to guess at what thoughts were moving through his mind. Then he said softly, 'As you're well aware I cannot afford to have people interfering in whatever plans I make.'

He broke off and said something to the driver. We were travelling along a narrow country road miles from anywhere. The next moment the driver spun the wheel and we turned off onto an uneven track littered with small stones and leaves that had already fallen from the overhanging trees.

There was a small building of some kind at the very end. It looked abandoned as if it had stood there for decades just whiling away its remaining years in a state of increasing disrepair. The car pulled up in front of it.

A moment later the two bruisers got out. The door on my side of the car was opened and hands reached inside, pulling me out. I stood swaying for a moment, blinking against the strong sunlight, sucking lungfuls of air through my open mouth.

Just before one of the men closed the limousine door, I heard Manzelli say in that soft, menacing voice of his:

'Goodbye, Mister Merak. I don't think we shall meet again.'

3

Death Takes A Step Back

One of the guys pushed the door open while the other pinned my arms behind my back and hustled me inside. From the large boxes stacked along one wall I guessed the place was a storage building of some kind; one possibly used for keeping various types of contraband away from the eyes of the cops.

There was one small window but it was so thickly smeared with dust that it allowed very little light into the place.

'Sorry it has to end this way, Merak,' sneered the guy at my back. 'But you've poked your nose into our business for the last time.'

'Sure you're sorry,' I replied. 'But not as sorry as you will be once the Feds catch up with you.'

They both laughed. Even I could see the joke.

The bigger guy came to a halt in front of me. His tobacco-stained teeth showed in a wide grin. I still had the .38 in its holster but there was no chance of reaching it. His friend had my arms held tightly at my back and there was no way of getting out of that grip.

Both of these men were professionals. They knew exactly what they were doing. Drawing back his right arm, the big guy threw a punch that landed just beneath my breastbone, knocking all of the wind out of my lungs. Gasping, I hung there as a second blow slammed against the side of my head.

My knees went but the man behind me continued to hold me up as more blows hammered at my face and chest. I could see the darkness closing in on me and there was the salty taste of blood in my mouth.

'That's enough,' muttered the guy at my back. 'Finish him off and let's get out of here.' He released his hold on my arms and I fell back, hitting my skull on the hard stone floor. Through the haze of pain I saw the hood standing in front of me. I seemed to be seeing things happening in slow motion.

He reached inside his jacket and pulled out a gun aiming it directly at my chest. I tried to roll out of the way but my legs and arms wouldn't move. Still smiling, he pulled the trigger. I saw a spurt of blue flame. There was a sharp pain on my left side — and then the blackness swallowed me up completely.

* * *

Coming out of that all-enveloping darkness was a long and agonizing process. Gradually, however, my mind began to function. I realized I couldn't be dead because I was lying on something hard. There was a dull pain everywhere in my body. It was only with a determined effort that I opened my eyes and forced them to stay open. Waves of agony pierced my left shoulder.

Little bits of confused memory began to come back to me. I vividly recalled the hood standing over me with a gun pointed at me. I had seen the muzzle flash and knew he had pulled the trigger. So why wasn't I dead? At that range it would have been impossible to miss.

Yet I could see. I could feel the rough floor pressing hard against my shoulder blades. Groaning with the pain, I succeeded in pushing myself into a sitting position. The only light in the place was the pale sunlight that struggled to pierce the thick layer of dirt on the window. Very slowly, I eased my jacket away from my left side. It was then that I saw what had miraculously saved my life.

There was a ragged abrasion along my shoulder holster. The slug intended for my heart had hit the hard metal of the .38 and ricocheted away, nicking the flesh. The wound was still bleeding a little, staining my shirt. The rest of me ached as if I'd been attacked by a maddened bull.

Evidently, I told myself, Saint Peter wasn't quite ready for me. But I was still in trouble. I'd no idea where I was and that car had certainly brought me quite a way before arriving at this place. With an effort, I got to my feet, clawing for the nearby wall. There was a carousel going round and round inside my head and I was going round with it.

I waited until the spinning sensation stopped. My stomach felt sore and queasy at the same time. But at least I was still alive. Now all I had to do was find my way back to town and that wasn't going to be easy. Somehow, I staggered to the door. It was locked. Apparently they didn't intend me to be found for some time.

I was in no position to kick the door down so I did the next best thing. Taking out the .38, I sent two shots into the lock. Going outside, I noticed there was no sign of the car. By now Manzelli would be miles away, back at his place on the other side of town.

The sun was already going down. Soon it would be dark and since the sky was clear it was also going to be cold. I started walking. I must have looked a pitiable sight staggering over the rough ground, weaving erratically from side to side. The sun went down twenty minutes later.

Somehow, I was still on my feet, still walking. The pain in my shoulder where the slug had just missed any vital parts, had subsided into a dull ache but my head was still throbbing and there was dry blood on the side of my face. That hoodlum had had fists like rocks and my jaw felt swollen from the beating I'd had.

Every nerve and muscle in my body was telling me it was foolish to keep going like this. I should stop and rest until I felt in better shape. But I knew that if I once stopped and sat down, I'd never get to my feet again. I had to keep moving no matter what it took. By the time it was fully dark I'd reached the end of the rough track and was walking along the side of a major road. I was still miles from anywhere with no sign of life showing in any direction.

Stopping for a moment, I tried to see what time it was, holding the watch close to my eyes and trying to make out the positions of the luminous hands but they didn't seem to make sense. I ran my thumb over the front, almost cutting myself on a jagged edge. The watch had stopped and I guessed it must have smashed when I hit the floor what

71

seemed an eternity earlier.

Sucking in a deep breath that hurt my chest, I started out again and it was at that moment that I picked up a sound; the first noise I'd heard since regaining consciousness. I stopped and turned slowly. There were lights some distance away and they seemed to come closer with every passing second. I couldn't make out what kind of vehicle it was but it was my only chance of getting out of that godforsaken place.

Keeping to the side of the road, I waited, one hand raised. I saw the car slow as the driver picked me out in the powerful headlights. It was a Cadillac and it stopped immediately opposite me.

The door opened and a woman's voice said, 'What under the stars happened to you?'

Wincing a little, I said, 'I guess you could say that some guys didn't like my face.'

She didn't laugh. Instead she said, 'You'd better get in and I'll drive you to a hospital.'

I walked around the car and slid in

beside her. I could just make out her features in the dimness. Around thirty-five, I guessed, well dressed, evidently a woman who had plenty of dough. Long blonde hair hung in waves over her shoulders.

For a moment I wondered what she was doing driving alone in the dark, picking up strangers who looked as if they'd been through the mill.

I figured that maybe she was a widow, or divorced, living on her own, still craving the company she'd once had. Closing the door, I settled back as she engaged the gears and set off. Whoever she was I certainly wasn't going to turn down an offer of a lift.

After a moment, I said, 'I don't need a doctor. This kind of thing happens to me all the time.'

If she was surprised by that remark, she didn't show it. Instead, she said, 'Then is there any place I can drop you, Mister — ?'

'Merak. Johnny Merak. I'm a private detective.' I gave her Dawn's address.

She mulled that over for a moment and

then smiled. 'And this address? Somehow I doubt if it's your own. Which is it — that of your wife, or your lover?'

'She's my partner in the crime business,' I replied.

'I see.' For a moment, she took her eyes off the road to stare straight at me. 'But you haven't asked my name yet.'

'I'm sorry. It's just that I've been punched and shot at, left for dead, and forced to walk for miles. My brain isn't thinking straight at the moment.'

She laughed softly. 'I understand. It's Zelda Marshall. I own a chain of boutiques in town.'

'Then I guess I owe you a lot, Zelda,' I said. 'If you should ever need the services of a private eye you can have them for free.' I gave her my business card.

'Thanks. I'll remember that.'

'Does your — partner in crime — know you're staying out late? She'll certainly be wondering where I am and what's happened.'

A couple of heavy freight trucks roared past us, their headlights dazzling in the darkness. It had begun to rain and she switched on the windscreen wipers.

'What exactly did happen?' she asked after a brief pause.

'You ask a lot of questions, lady,' I said. For some odd reason those little mice were beginning to run around inside my mind. I couldn't help listening to them. They were saying that, perhaps, it was more than a coincidence that this dame happened to be travelling along that road at just the time I was on it.

I tried to tell myself that I was imagining things now. There was no way Zelda could have known what had taken place and had been there according to some prearranged plan with Manzelli at the back of it. Yet that thought persisted in spite of all I could do to push it out of my mind.

She gave a shrug. 'Sorry. I didn't mean to pry into your private life. I was just making conversation although I'll admit that you interest me. I don't often pick up strangers who look as though they've just gone ten rounds with some heavyweight wrestler. I hope you're not offended.'

'No.' I shook my head. 'No offence

taken. All that happened was that I was picked up in town and driven out to some deserted shack in the middle of nowhere. It seems I've trodden on their toes a little while investigating a case.'

'One of them catch you out, sleeping with his wife?'

'Nothing like that. I guess I was getting just a little close to the truth and he didn't want that to come out into the open. So he decided to get some thugs to beat me up and make sure I kept quiet.'

We were now approaching the outskirts of town and here she had to concentrate on driving. There was now a lot more late-night traffic around and at times I had to give her directions. Finally, however, she stopped outside Dawn's apartment.

There was a light in the window. I knew that she would have waited for me to show up at the office. When I didn't she would have locked up and gone home, doubtless wondering where I was and what sort of mess I'd got myself into.

Opening the car door, I got out. 'Thanks once again for the lift, Zelda,' I said. 'It's possible we may meet again.'

'I hope so too. I look forward to it.'

I closed the door. She gave me a little wave and then drove off into the night. I watched her tail lights vanish around the far corner and then went up to Dawn's door.

It opened just before I reached it. She took one look at me and then grabbed my arm and pulled me inside, closing the door behind me. 'What in God's name happened to you, Johnny? You leave in the middle of the day without a word and I'm left in the office thinking the worst.'

'It's a long story, Dawn. I think I can tell it better after a drink.'

I sat down in the chair near the fire as she crossed to the small cabinet. Over her shoulder, she asked, 'And who was the dame in the car? Another client?'

'Not exactly. Just a friendly motorist who happened to pick me up miles out of town.'

A pause, then, 'Not too friendly, I hope.'

'You think I'd be up for anything like that in my condition?'

'No. I guess that not even you would try anything like that in your present state.' She came back with the drink and went down onto her knees in front of me. 'What really happened, Johnny? You look a mess. Drink that and then I'll help you clean up.'

I took a few sips of the straight bourbon. It tasted good and brought some of the feeling back into my battered body. 'It seems I've trodden on someone's toes and he doesn't like it.'

'Whose toes are they?' She spoke in a hushed tone as if dreading what the answer would be.

'Manzelli.'

She pulled her head back as if someone had just slapped her in the face. 'Manzelli! But I thought you were on fairly good terms with him.'

'So did I. But it seems I've stirred up a real hornet's nest taking on Dexter as a client. I don't know what's at the back of Manzelli's mind but he wants me out of the game — just how permanently, I don't know.'

She got slowly to her feet and began

pacing up and down the room. 'You'd better tell me all that's happened from the beginning.'

I waited until she'd poured a second drink into my glass, lit a cigarette, and then told her as many details as I could remember. When I'd finished, her face had assumed a scared expression. Sinking down into the other chair, she sat staring at me.

Finally, she said, 'What are you going to do now, Johnny? It won't be long before Manzelli finds out that you're still alive.'

'All I can do is let things take their course.' I finished my drink. 'Right now, all I want is to sleep the clock around.'

'I'll get you some things while you wash some of that blood off your face. Then you can sleep as long as you like.'

When I woke the next morning the early morning sunlight was streaming in through the window. My face was still swollen and I still looked a mess but the pain was subsiding. Dawn was nowhere to be seen but there was the smell of hot coffee coming from the direction of the kitchen.

My clothes were folded neatly over the

back of a chair. I dressed quickly and went downstairs. She was sitting at the small table staring out of the window. From the expression on her face I figured she expected to see half a dozen hoods suddenly pop up at any moment in the street outside.

She got up when I entered and went over to the cooker. 'Do you feel like eating anything, Johnny?' she asked.

'I feel famished,' I told her, sitting down.

'I gather it won't be wise to go back to the office,' she said as she placed a plate of fried bacon and eggs in front of me.

'That's what I've been thinking about,' I replied between mouthfuls. 'I've been in this position before with the entire Organization on my back. They haven't got rid of me yet and I'm damned if I'm going to hide from them.'

'But if Manzelli — ' she began, pouring out some coffee.

'That's what I've been going over in my mind ever since I woke up. There was something strange about the whole set-up yesterday, something I can't put my finger on.'

She glanced up from her plate. 'What do you mean, Johnny? There doesn't seem any doubt Manzelli meant to have you killed.'

'That's what I don't get. Firstly, Manzelli never leaves that place of his. He wants somebody killed and the order goes out from there. This time he came in person and that's totally out of character for the guy. It was as if he wanted to give me a big scare and a going-over — and that was all. Somehow, I got the feeling that he came to make sure that was carried out.'

'But you claim that hoodlum deliberately shot you. If you're saying that that bullet wasn't meant to kill you, you're just deluding yourself.'

'Oh, that guy meant to kill me, all right. But I don't think that was what Manzelli had in mind. That bruiser must've had some kind of grudge against me, probably from the old days, and saw an opportunity to get even. And there's another thing. Manzelli's no fool. Why didn't his boys frisk me and take away my gun?'

'I don't know. But at the moment you

seem to be finding excuses for Manzelli not wanting to kill you.'

'Well there's only one way to find out. As far as I'm concerned, it's business as usual.'

Dawn reached a decision. 'Then if that's what you're going to do, I'm coming in with you.'

We got to the office half an hour later. There was someone standing in front of the door waiting for us. It was O'Leary and he was without his shadow, Sergeant Kolowinski.

Opening the door, I let him go in first. Tossing my hat onto the peg on the wall, I sat down, facing him across the desk.

'I thought I'd come and tell you that you're no longer a suspect in Sergei Karmov's murder,' he said. 'We managed to find a witness who corroborates your story. We've also located what we're sure is the murder weapon. The forensic team are examining it right now.'

'What was it?' I asked.

'A .22. Once we check the bullets, we'll know for sure.'

'Where did you find it?'

'More than half a mile away. Hidden in some thick undergrowth.'

I gave a grim smile. 'And I'm equally sure you'll find no prints.'

O'Leary ran his gaze over my face. He seemed to have noticed the bruises for the first time. 'What the hell happened to you?'

'A little disagreement with a few of my old friends from the Organization,' I told him. 'Seems they don't like the way I'm going about things.'

'I always said you'd get yourself into big trouble one of these days.'

'Well, Lieutenant, you know me. Johnny Merak goes where angels fear to tread.'

'You'll do that once too often and we'll have to drag you off the bottom of the ocean.'

He pushed back his chair and got up. 'Well, that's all I came to tell you — except to warn you once again to keep your nose out of police matters.'

'You won't stay for a cup of coffee, Lieutenant?' Dawn asked.

'Some of us have important work to

do,' he muttered and went out.

'He doesn't sound very happy,' Dawn remarked. She riffled through the stack of notes on her desk. 'While you were getting yourself beaten to a pulp yesterday I wasn't exactly idle. I went along to Dexter's casino on Sunset Strip. I left a note in case you came back and wondered where I'd got to.'

'You went to that place?'

'That's right. I thought that if I snooped around a bit I might see or hear something important.'

'And did you?'

'There was one odd thing that happened.'

'What was that?'

'Malloy arrived with those two minders of his. They went straight into Dexter's office and stayed there for almost an hour. I managed to work my way across the room without being spotted and stood just outside the door.'

'Did you hear anything?'

She shook her head. 'I couldn't make out any of the words except that once, Malloy shouted 'Why the hell did you let him do it?' Or something very like that.'

'Would you say it was an amicable meeting?'

'Far from it. Their voices were raised virtually all of the time and Malloy's face was like thunder when he came out.'

I didn't know what to think of this information. The only conclusion I could reach was that Malloy had carried out his threat and gone to warn Dexter to keep in line. He and Dexter had never been on good terms. On a few occasions when Sharky's place had been raided by the cops it had been rumoured that Malloy had been the one who'd given the nod to the police.

I was still trying to figure it out ten minutes later when the phone rang. It was the last person in the world I expected to be calling me. Enrico Manzelli!

'I think I should clear up one little misunderstanding about yesterday,' he began. 'It was never my intention to have you killed. You can still be of use to me. That is why I didn't have you eliminated altogether. I'm sure you'll be pleased to learn that the man who disobeyed my strict instructions and pulled that gun on you is no longer in my employ.'

Knowing Manzelli of old, I knew exactly what he meant by that last remark. That hoodlum who had pointed the gun at me and pulled the trigger was no longer among the living. It was as simple as that.

'I guess I should thank you for that,' I said. 'Although I'm still in the dark about what I'm supposed to have done.'

There was the sound of a dry chuckle at the other end of the line. 'I have my own plans for Dexter and your, rather precipitous, action in working on his behalf has upset those plans a little. However, I'm sure that you'll do your best to rectify matters. What happened yesterday was to keep you in check and act as a reminder that no one steps out of line. I trust you understand that.'

'I understand perfectly,' I said dryly. I was still feeling a deep-seated anger at the way I'd been beaten up but where Manzelli was concerned, I knew it was better to keep my mouth shut.

'Excellent. Now listen carefully. I can't

afford any further mistakes. Something is taking place among certain of the outfits about which I know little. I want you to find out what it is. As far as I know, it all began with that curious affair at Dexter's casino. What happened that night was, on the face of it, impossible. It should never have happened.

'By now, you probably know that Dexter and Malloy are in on something together. My guess is they're plotting against me and trying to undermine my authority. If they are, then I shall have to take the appropriate action — but first I have to be absolutely certain. You are going to find out for me exactly what is going on between them.'

'All right.' My throat felt suddenly dry. 'I'll do my best.'

'Just be sure that it is your best.' The line went dead as he put the phone down.

As I replaced the receiver Dawn asked, 'Who was that, Johnny?'

'I'll give you three guesses.'

'Oh God, not Manzelli?'

'I'm afraid so. At least I'm off the hook as far as he's concerned. There's no hit out on me. But he seems certain that Malloy and Dexter are cooking up something against him and it's up to me to find out what it is. Apparently he reckons it all started with that joker winning all that dough by betting on thirteen three times.'

'Are you going to do what he asks?'

I forced a wry grin. 'Manzelli never asks, Dawn, he demands. He's got this entire city in his pocket from the top politicians and cops to the ordinary guy in the street.'

'So what he says bears out what I saw yesterday? That meeting between those two.'

'It would certainly seem so. That doesn't worry me. What does is why Sergei Karmov was killed and who did it. I'm sure his murder is tied in with all of this.'

'So how are you going to find out any more about that? O'Leary won't tell you anything.'

'No, but Jack Kolowinski might.' I checked my watch. 'He may be off duty at the moment. If he is, I know exactly where to find him.'

Mancini's was open as usual when I got there. There were very few customers but Kolowinski was there, holding up the bar. I walked over and sat on the vacant stool beside him. His glass was almost empty.

I waited until he drained it and then signalled to the barkeep to bring a couple more. 'So what goes with Karmov's murder, Jack?' I asked. 'Has O'Leary got any further with the case?'

'I thought you were off the case now he's dead.'

'I'd like to be,' I replied. 'But you know me. If there are any loose ends lying around I like to tidy them up. It's too easy to trip over them.'

'We got one tip yesterday. I don't know what it means but apparently that guy Karmov was seen in conversation with some woman less than an hour before you discovered his body. According to our witness they appeared to be having quite a violent argument.'

'Do you have any description of this woman?'

He tipped his glass and half of the whiskey went down his throat as if dropping into a well. 'Sure. She was apparently quite tall, well-dressed, aged around thirty-five with long blonde hair. It could fit thousands of women in L.A.'

I felt a little tingle along my spine. Those little mice were shouting at me now, telling me it could also fit the woman who'd picked me up the previous night. It might have been a coincidence but I don't believe in coincidences. Cause and effect was my philosophy.

Little bits of the puzzle were beginning to drop into place but I didn't really like the picture that was emerging. Maybe Manzelli was right and there was someone trying to usurp his position as the Big Boss. There were still a lot of individual strands that had to be drawn together if they were to make any kind of sense but at least I now had a new lead.

If this dame, Zelda Marshall, was in some way tied in with the Karmov brothers it shouldn't be too difficult to find the connection. She already told me she owned a chain of boutiques in the city. I figured that was a job for Dawn.

After getting the bartender to refill Kolowinski's glass, I left Mancini's and went straight back to the office. Dawn was still there.

'Did you find out anything?' she asked as I sat down.

'It may be something or nothing,' I told her. 'Jack reckons that some witness saw a blonde dame having some kind of argument with Sergei some time before his body was found. The funny thing is her description fits that of the dame who gave me a lift yesterday.'

'Do you know who she is?'

I nodded. 'She told me her name was Zelda Marshall and she owns a string of boutiques.'

'And you want me to find out something about her?'

'That's right. If she is the same woman, then her picking me up last night was no coincidence. She must have known who I was and I'd be somewhere on that road. At the moment, I've no idea where she fits into all this.'

'In the meantime I think I'll have another talk with Dexter. I may be able to get a few leads on whether he is in with Malloy.'

4

Dark Secrets

The minute I entered Dexter's casino I knew there was something wrong. Most of the tables were empty and a small crowd had gathered near the door that led into Sharky's office. At first, I couldn't see anything out of the ordinary and then I noticed the thin wisp of grey-white smoke that was seeping through beneath the door.

Someone was shouting, 'He's still in there! For God's sake get the cops and the fire service. We'll need an ambulance too.'

A woman was screaming somewhere on the far side of the room. There was another mass exodus towards the street. I knew there could be only one person trapped inside that office, Sharky Dexter — and I wanted to talk to him. Dead, he was no use to me. I didn't wait to think.

Hauling a couple of guys out of the way I took a run at the door and slammed into it with my shoulder.

It gave slightly but that was all. I tried again and this time it crashed open. A gush of flame and heat came out. Through the smoke I could just make out the figure lying on the floor a couple of feet from the desk. Flames were everywhere.

Without thinking, I ran inside. Behind me, a woman yelled something. A little voice inside my head said that this was the most stupid thing I had done in my life. Somehow, I got my hands under his shoulders and pulled.

Tears and smoke were blinding me. The heat was scorching my face. Then I was outside and somebody took Dexter from me and hauled him further away from the door. A big guy, I figured he was one of the employees, thumped me on the back and thrust something into my hand.

'Here, buster,' he said. 'Take this. It's on the house.'

I looked down at it. Somehow, through the veil of tears I recognized what it was.

A glass of bourbon. Clutching it tightly as if it were the Crown Jewels of England, I made it to a chair. My mouth and throat were as dry as the sands of Arabia but somehow I got the drink down.

A couple of minutes later the cops and an ambulance arrived, together with the guys from the fire service. Sharky looked dreadful, his clothing blackened by the fire, but he was still breathing as they piled him onto a stretcher and carried him out.

Someone in the crowd said something to one of the doctors and he walked over to me. 'They tell me you went in and dragged him out,' he said. 'That was a damn-fool thing to do.'

'How is he?' My voice was little more than a croak.

'He'll make it. Second degree burns to parts of his body. Smoke inhalation. We'll get him to the hospital. Is he a friend of yours?'

'An acquaintance,' I corrected him. 'I need to talk to him as soon as he's well enough.'

'That won't be for a week or so, I'm

afraid. But I think we ought to get you to hospital too. Just for a check up,'

'I'm O.K. doc.'

'You don't look O.K. to me. Now — '

Before he could say anything more another guy came up. I could tell just by looking at him that he was a cop before he showed his badge. 'Lieutenant Denman,' he said in clipped tones, the kind that told you he meant to have no nonsense. He looked directly at me. 'What happened here?'

I shook my head slowly. 'Obviously someone started a fire in that room. It was well alight when I got here. The door was locked and there was smoke coming from under it.'

'You're certain the door was locked?'

'Of course I'm certain. I nearly busted my shoulder knocking it in.'

'So it seems obvious that someone tried to murder him.'

I nodded. 'I'd say that's a fairly sound conclusion.'

He wasn't sure whether I was agreeing with him or being sarcastic but he let it pass. 'What's your name?'

'I thought you were never going to ask, Lieutenant,' I said and this time there was deliberate sarcasm in my voice. I took out my business card and handed it to him.

He scanned it slowly and meticulously as if trying to absorb every single word. Then he gave it back. 'So you're Merak. I've heard of you from Lieutenant O'Leary.'

'I'll bet you have.'

'It seems you don't care much for the way the police do their work. You reckon you're better at detective work than we are?'

I shrugged. 'Who knows? I've solved a few murder cases that had O'Leary stumped.'

'Sure. The trouble is that you tend to step over the line and slip back into the old ways of the Mobs.'

'I've known some cops do that,' I replied, standing up. I placed the empty glass on the table. 'Is there anything more you need me for, Lieutenant?'

He deliberated for a moment and then shook his head. 'I know where to find you, Merak, if I have any more questions to ask you.'

I went outside. The ambulance with Sharky in it was already screaming away, its siren blaring. I'd hoped to ask him some really important questions but someone had got to him first. Fortunately, if the killer didn't manage to sneak into the hospital and complete the job, I might still be able to get something out of him.

The office was empty when I arrived. I considered making myself a mug of strong black coffee but then figured that I needed something stronger. Opening the drawer of the desk I took out the half-empty bottle of Scotch and a glass. Pouring some of the whiskey into the glass I tilted my chair back and placed my feet on the desk.

A lot of things were happening now and some of them weren't going the way I'd have liked. Manzelli was convinced that Dexter and Malloy were working together. Since he'd told me to find out just what was going on, it seemed unlikely he'd have Dexter killed before I could get some answers.

That could mean only one thing.

Somewhere out there was a killer who had already murdered twice and had almost succeeded with Dexter. It was then I remembered the stiff I'd found in Igor Karmov's place. Where did he fit into the puzzle? All I knew about him was that he'd been part of Malloy's outfit.

I'd fitted together a few bits of the jigsaw but these formed only the edges. The area in the middle, the really important bit, was still a blank. Before I could drive myself crazy trying to figure things out, the door opened and Dawn came in.

She glanced disapprovingly at the glass in my hand and then she noticed the burn marks on my face and said, 'You look a mess, Johnny. What happened to your face?'

'Someone tried to kill Dexter by setting fire to his office and locking him inside,' I told her.

'And of course, you had to go in and get him out. Guys like that deserve all they get.'

'Sure. But I didn't intend to have him die on me before I got some answers.'

She shook her head in exasperation.

'One of these days you're going to get yourself killed acting the hero.'

She came over and sat on the desk beside me. 'Let me take a look at those burns.'

Her hands felt cool on my face. 'I think you've done enough for today, Johnny. Once we get to my place I'll fix you up. If anyone rings here, they'll have to wait until tomorrow.'

'What about the low-down on Zelda Marshall?'

'I'll give you all the details I've got on her later.' There was a note of finality in her tone and I knew better than to argue. Dawn insisted on attending to the burns on my face and then cooking us something to eat before giving me what information she'd got on Zelda Marshall. Not until we were settled in front of the electric fire did she bring out the pad on which she had written her notes.

'Apparently her real name is Elizabeth Marshall but once she started up her business she changed it to Zelda. Originally she came from some out-of-the-way place in southern Arizona. I managed to check her bank accounts. At the time she came to L.A. she had hardly any money but then, almost overnight, she had this flourishing chain of boutiques.'

'How the hell did you get that information? I thought it was supposed to be confidential,' I interjected.

She smiled. 'I said I was a journalist and we were writing an article on her for one of the big magazines.'

'And they gave you that information?'

'Flutter your eyelashes at some of these older men and they'll do anything for you.'

'I can imagine,' I interjected. 'So someone obviously bankrolled her.'

'It would seem so,' Dawn acknowledged without looking up from the notebook balanced on one knee.

'Go on.' I guessed there was more to come.

'I tried to find out if she's connected with any of the outfits in L.A. but if there is one she's been very clever at concealing it. However, I visited one of her shops and made some discreet inquiries among the staff. Believe me, Johnny, you'd be surprised at some of the gossip you can pick up from her employees.'

'Jealous of her success?' I suggested.

'That — and her general attitude towards them.'

'Meaning she wasn't much liked?'

'Exactly.'

'That could mean that anything detrimental they said about her might be exaggerated. It may be difficult to separate the truth from lies.'

Dawn pursed her lips. 'That's true, I suppose. But there was talk from quite a number of them that she's been seen several times in the company of Michael Florencio.'

That was something I hadn't been expecting. Florencio was one of Joe Malloy's top men — a slick, smooth operator. He always tried to give the impression of being a perfect gentleman. But beneath his suave exterior was a ruthless killer with a heart of solid stone. He'd been taken in for suspected murder on at least three occasions but the charges had never stuck.

'So there may be a tie-up with the Organization here,' I said.

'Perhaps he's her pot of gold,' Dawn suggested. 'The guy she got all the money from to start up her business.'

I yawned. The heat from the fire was making me drowsy. The pain in my face was subsiding a little. 'We'll go through it all again tomorrow,' I said. 'Just in case there's anything important we've missed.'

We went over everything again the next morning over breakfast but it seemed we'd got all of the information there was to be had on Zelda Marshall. We were on the point of leaving for the office when Dawn's phone rang. She looked at me with a puzzled expression, evidently not expecting anyone to call.

Lifting the receiver she spoke into it for a moment; then handed it to me. 'It's for you, Johnny. A woman who wants to speak to you urgently.'

I took it from her. 'Merak,' I said.

A voice that I couldn't place said, 'Remember me, Johnny? You told me that if I ever needed the services of a private investigator you'd give them for free.'

'Zelda?'

'The very same. I have to see you as soon as possible.'

'How did you get this number?'

She laughed softly. 'It wasn't difficult. I drove you to that address — remember? I simply checked with the phone company. I have my connections.'

'I see. Well, I'm on my way to the office at this very moment. Do you know where it is?'

'I can find it.'

'Then I'll expect you in half an hour.'

I gave the phone back to Dawn. 'Zelda Marshall,' I told her. 'It would seem she has ways of getting to know everything. She'll be at the office in half an hour.'

Replacing the receiver, Dawn said sharply, 'This seems to be too much of a coincidence.'

She was right. I had the feeling I was caught in the middle of a web and the strands were drawing tighter by the minute.

Precisely half an hour later there was a soft knock on the office door and she came in. She sat down in the chair opposite and crossed her legs. Taking a cigarette from a gold case, she placed it between her lips and inclined her head towards me as I leaned over the desk and flicked my lighter. I knew Dawn was watching me closely from the other side of the room.

'May I ask the nature of your problem?' I sat back and watched her closely.

She opened the expensive handbag and brought out a folded piece of paper. 'I received this through my letterbox this morning. I think you'll see at once why I'm worried.' She handed it to me across the desk.

Smoothing it out in front of me I saw that it was a warning made up of letters cut from a number of newspapers and glossy magazines. The wording was stark, simple and to the point. It said: *Say your prayers. You die two days after tomorrow.*

'Do you have any idea at all who would want to send you this?' I asked.

She shook her head. 'I can't think of anyone who hates me so much. I've trodden on a few toes to get where I am today. But that's the way it is in any business.'

'It could be even nearer home than that,' Dawn put in from the other side of the room.

Zelda looked round sharply, surprise on her face. 'What do you mean by that?' she demanded heatedly.

'I was in one of your departments yesterday and heard some of the staff talking among themselves. It seems you've been seeing quite a lot of a certain Michael Florencio recently.'

'So what if I have? I fail to see what my private life, and who I see, has to do either with you — or this case.'

'It's possible that Florencio may have quite a lot to do with it, Zelda,' I interjected.

She pressed her lips into a straight, angry line. It took away some of the beauty of her features. 'Why do you say that? You think you know him better than I do?'

'I know he's one of the top men running Joe Malloy's outfit,' I replied. 'He's been charged with murder three times but each time some slick city lawyer got him off the hook.'

'Have you considered that that was because he didn't commit them?'

'Sure. And the British won the War of Independence.'

That stung her to the core. Her face flared a deep crimson and she got off her chair so quickly I thought she'd knock the desk over. 'I see it was a big mistake to come and ask for your help, Mister Merak,' she said heatedly. 'I think I'll hire myself another lawyer, one who might be of some help.' Spinning on her heel she went out, slamming the door behind her.

'Don't you think you were a little hard on her, Johnny?' Dawn asked.

'Not at all. If she believes that Michael Florencio is the Archangel Gabriel then she's a very deluded woman.'

'Perhaps. But I'd say you've made an enemy there.'

I grinned. 'Enemies I can handle. It's the so-called friends I have to watch out for.'

Dawn was silent for a moment and then asked, 'So what can we do now? We seem to have exhausted everyone we can question.'

'All except one.'

'Oh? Who's that?'

'Sharky Dexter. I'd like to hear what he has to say about that fire at the casino. It's possible he saw who started it.'

'This time I'm coming with you,' she said in that tone of voice that told me not to argue with her. 'Everywhere you go you seem to get into some kind of trouble.'

'All right,' I agreed. 'I don't think anything can happen in the hospital.'

Once there we found ourselves confronted by the usual no-nonsense receptionist. She glared at me as if wondering how I dared to come into the hospital asking to see one of the patients.

'Who is it you wish to see?' she demanded, glancing down at the book in front of her.

'Mister Dexter,' I told her.

'Are you relatives or close friends of his?'

I shrugged. 'Somehow I doubt if he has any relatives or close friends.'

She looked up from the book. 'Mister

Dexter has asked that no one should be allowed in to see him.'

'Perhaps if you were to give him my business card he might change his mind.' I gave it to her.

She took it and studied it as if examining every single letter through a microscope. 'Very well,' she said grudgingly, 'But he left strict orders he wasn't to be disturbed by anyone.'

She called someone else to watch the desk and marched off along a corridor. While we waited, I asked the second woman, 'Do you know how Mister Dexter is today. When I last saw him he didn't look too well.'

Leaning forward as if imparting some deep, dark secret, she said in a low voice, 'I believe he has second degree burns to several areas of his body. He was lucky that his face wasn't touched.'

'I reckon it wouldn't have made much difference where Sharky is concerned,' I muttered. Dawn gave me a disapproving look at that remark.

The receptionist made to say something more but at that moment the first woman returned.

She looked disappointed by whatever news she'd been given. 'The doctor says you may see him for ten minutes but no longer. He's in the private ward at the far end of the corridor.' She pointed along the way she'd come.

'Thank you,' Dawn said sweetly. The look she got should have fried her on the spot.

Dexter was lying in the bed with his head propped up on two thick pillows. He didn't look too pleased to see us but at least he didn't tell us to go away. His hands were bandaged and I guessed much of his body was the same.

'How are you feeling, Sharky?' I asked.

He grimaced as he tried to push himself up in the bed. 'Are you trying to be funny, Merak?' he snapped.

'Not at all. I came along to see if you're up to answering a few questions.'

'Do I look as if I'm fit for an interrogation?' He pushed his head deeper into the pillows. 'Still, they tell me you risked your life to save me so I guess I owe you something.'

There were a couple of chairs, one on either side of the bed, and we sat down.

'What the hell happened in your office, Sharky?' I asked. 'It's obvious someone is out to kill you. Do you have any idea who it is?'

'Do you think he'd still be walking the streets if I knew who it is? All I know is that I was at the wall safe when someone came in. The next thing I'm out like a light. I don't know a thing after that until I woke up in this joint, bandaged like a damned Egyptian mummy.'

'Whoever it was he certainly didn't mean you to come round and get out. The door was locked and I had to bust it in.'

Dexter considered that for a full two minutes and then muttered, 'Then it looks as though you've got another job to do for me, Merak. Find out who it was and then let me know right away.' He held up a bandaged hand as I made to protest. 'I won't take no for an answer. There's another ten grand in it for you once you give me his name.'

'O.K. I'll try. But before we go, do you

111

know anything about a woman who calls herself Zelda Marshall and a guy she's seeing — Michael Florencio?'

I knew by the sudden look in his eyes that he was well acquainted with at least one of them. 'Why are you asking about them? You think they could figure somewhere in this case?'

'It's possible,' I admitted. 'At the moment I seem to be coming up against nothing but dead ends. No one appears to know anything — or if they do, they're clamming up and not talking.'

'Florencio is the guy who runs most of all the casinos Malloy has. I have the rest including most of the biggest. He's been coming on to me for the past couple of years, telling me to sell up and take what he calls a well-earned rest.'

'Meaning that he's trying to push you out and get your share of the gambling market?'

'Can you think of any other reason?'

I couldn't so I asked, 'Has he made any threats against you?'

He shook his head. 'Not exactly unless — ' He paused as a fresh thought struck him, ' — unless he's the one who tried to kill me.'

I sat back in the chair. My mind seemed to be running off along tangents now. I knew Malloy had always wanted to expand his empire in L.A. On a number of occasions he'd tried to grab some territory from the other big outfit run by Sam Rizzio.

There were a few other questions I wanted to ask him. But at that moment this guy comes in. He was dressed in a white coat and had a stethoscope draped around his neck.

'I'm sorry but I'm afraid I must ask you to leave now,' he said. 'My patient needs as much rest as possible.'

I got up. From the bed, Sharky said thinly, 'Remember to do that little job for me, Johnny. Don't forget.'

'I won't,' I told him as we went out. At the reception desk the dame threw me a look of naked hostility as we passed. I guessed she figured her authority had been undermined and she didn't like it.

The car park was full when we got there. I'd parked the Merc some distance from the entrance. Taking the keys from my pocket I made to insert it in the lock, then stopped. Something hard was jammed against the bottom of my spine.

'You won't be needing your car, Merak,' said a cold, metallic voice. 'You're coming in ours. That goes for your lady friend too.'

I saw Dawn watching me from the other side of the car. There was a scared look on her face. A big guy was immediately behind her and I guessed he had a gun as well.

'All right. Move,' grunted the guy at my back. 'And don't try to make any funny moves. The boss would prefer us to take you alive but if you want it the other way I don't think he'll shed any tears.'

'And who is this boss of yours?' I asked as we were made to move towards the far side of the parking area.

The guy laughed. It wasn't a very nice sound. 'You'll find that out soon enough.'

The black limousine that seemed to be the trademark of the various outfits stood waiting for us. Dawn and I were pushed into the back. One of the guys got behind the wheel while the other sat beside him, covering us with the gun.

We drove off, out of the car park and then onto the main road, heading west. That told me at once that it wasn't Manzelli who wanted to see us. His place lay in the country several miles east of the city. At first, I thought that Sam Rizzio had put out the call, maybe wondering how I was tied in with Malloy.

But the way the car was now heading was down towards the beach. Some guy with a boat, I thought, waiting to take us out to the sea where we'd be dropped overboard at some convenient distance from the shore. It would be a long time, if ever, before our bodies were washed up.

'Look guys,' I said, breaking the long silence, 'If you let us know where we're going, I might be — '

'Just keep your mouth shut, Merak. We don't have far to go now. Then you'll learn everything.' He uttered that sniggering laugh again, sending little shivers along my spine.

The Pacific was now on our left, less than a quarter of a mile away. We were moving along a narrow cliff road, only slightly wider than the limousine. It angled sharply and there, high up, standing alone near the edge of the cliff, was a large mansion with white stone pillars in the old Colonial style favoured by the Big Boys in the Organization.

Evidently we were expected. The gates were open and we drove through, coming to a smooth halt near the front door. The guy in front got out, motioning with the gun for Dawn and I to do likewise.

'Inside,' he ordered in a voice like gravel.

One of the bruisers thrust open the door and led the way while his companion brought up the rear. There was no doubt that the top men in the Organization really did themselves well. Looking around me I noticed there were several paintings along the walls and I guessed they were all originals. These guys didn't go in for any fakes or second-hand stuff.

We went right to the end of the corridor. The big fellow knocked on the door twice and then waited. Someone shouted something from inside and we

116

went in. I gave the room a quick once-over.

A guy was sitting in a swivel chair behind the long mahogany desk, his back to us. The door behind us closed but I guessed that the two hatchet-men hadn't left. They were standing as quiet as mice at our backs.

Then the guy in the chair swung round to face us, placing his well-manicured hands in front of him. I knew him at once. Michael Florencio, top man and a ruthless killer, second only to Joe Malloy in the outfit.

In a voice that had a strange hiss to it, like that of a snake, he said, 'Please sit down, both of you.'

We did as we were told. Out of the corner of my eye I saw that my earlier surmise had been correct. The two gorillas that had brought us were still there, hands hanging loosely by their sides, ready to carry out any order that Florencio might give.

Florencio placed the tips of his fingers together and stared at us out of cold, emotionless eyes. I supposed the ladies would find him handsome with his black hair brushed straight back and dark Italian looks. Me — I knew him for what he was. Someone who often preferred to carry out his own executions himself rather than delegate them to any of his thugs.

'It has recently come to my attention that you've been taking a sudden interest in me, Merak,' he murmured thinly. 'That is something I don't like. However, I'm sure you can explain things to my satisfaction. If not, then you must suffer the consequences — both of you.'

I noticed how he stressed the last three words. They told me that Dawn and I were in really big trouble and it was not going to be easy to talk myself out of this situation.

Clearing my throat, I said as evenly as possible, 'I'm not sure where you got that information, Mister Florencio, but I can assure you that I have no interest at all in your activities.'

'No?'

'No, I will admit, however, that I have been asking about a friend of yours.'

His brows went up at that remark. 'A friend of mine?' he repeated. 'May I ask who that is?'

I hesitated. I knew I was taking both of our lives in my hands by telling him my interest in his girlfriend. It was extremely likely, knowing his violent temper, he would jump to the wrong conclusions.

'Zelda Marshall.'

I saw the knuckles of his hands whiten as he clenched them tightly into fists on the desk. Somehow, he controlled himself. 'What has Zelda got to do with anything?' His voice now had even more of a hissing quality to it. 'How did you meet her — and where?'

'It's a long story — ' I began.

'Then cut out the details and give me straight answers. You're beginning to bore me.' His glance flicked over our heads towards the two guys standing near the door behind us.

'A day or two ago, I was taken out to some shack miles outside of town by Manzelli and some of his boys. There they gave me a good going-over.'

Florencio's thin lips twitched into what

was meant to be a smile but failed miserably. 'So you've fallen foul of Manzelli. That's strange. The last I heard you were well in with him.'

'He just wanted to teach me a lesson, I guess,' I replied, 'I did something he didn't like. But it's all forgotten now. He rang me the next day and told me to do something for him.'

I slipped that bit of information in because I figured that Manzelli was still the Big Boss and Florencio wouldn't want to do anything that went against his wishes.

'Go on.'

'When his henchmen had finished they left me there. I reckoned the only way I'd get back to town would be to walk all the way. I was just making it along the road, still some miles out of town, when this car came along and the driver picked me up and gave me a lift into town. She told me her name was Zelda Marshall.'

'And that was the only time you've met her?'

I debated whether to lie to him, then decided to tell him everything. If Zelda talked, and he found out I'd lied to him, my life would come to an abrupt end in the most painful way.

'No. She came to my office yesterday asking for my help. Apparently she'd received a note telling her that she would die within two days. Unfortunately with the work I have to do for Manzelli I wasn't able to take her case at the time.'

'So you refused to help her?'

'There was nothing else I could do. I think you're aware that if you turn down an order from Manzelli you don't live long enough to regret it.'

Florencio's thin lips twitched into what was meant to be a smile. 'I don't believe a word you've said about just meeting her on the road, Merak. Not only that, however, but you seem to know far too much — and I do not approve of the way you spoke to Zelda the last time you met.'

He slid his glance in Dawn's direction. 'I've nothing personal against you, lady, but if you must consort with stupid men, you must suffer the consequences.'

'And you think that by getting rid of us you'll escape Manzelli's anger. The work he's asked me to do for him is extremely important and urgent. He won't be very pleased if I'm not around to do it.'

'Personally, it's of little interest to me what Manzelli thinks.' Florencio swung his chair so that his back was towards us again.

He waved an arm as if to indicate we were no longer of any consequence where he was concerned. Before either of us could move, the two strong-arm guys had grabbed our arms and hauled us to our feet.

The hoodlum at my back placed his arm across my chest and slid the .38 from its holster. Opening the door, they propelled us along the corridor and outside. At that moment the black limousine came around the corner of the house where it had obviously been waiting. It slid to a smooth stop in front of us. I noticed that the guy behind the wheel was a different one to the man who'd brought us.

His sharp angular features looked strangely familiar to me but I couldn't remember where I'd seen him before unless it was in the Comero Restaurant sitting beside Joe Malloy.

Dawn and I were bundled into the back. The hood with my gun sat beside me next to the car door. The second guy slipped in beside the driver.

'Now we'll all go for a little drive,' grated the man beside me. 'It's a pity the two of you won't be coming back.'

We drove out through the gates and then turned right in the direction of the ocean. I figured they'd already decided how we were to die. There'd be a motorboat or a yacht of some kind waiting at one of the small jetties along the coastline.

Once a couple of miles or so away from the coast we'd be tossed overboard with lead weights attached to our feet. It was quick, effective — and virtually painless. Maybe in a couple of weeks' time we'd be washed up along the shore and a few folk would wonder what had happened to us. But nobody would ask any questions.

About a mile along the narrow road we turned off onto a track that wound along the top of the cliff. I must say one thing, that driver certainly knew his job. He drove along the cliff edge, his face completely impassive, almost as if he were doing it in his sleep.

He eventually stopped at a spot where the track was a little wider than the rest and put on the handbrake.

'Here's where you get off,' grunted the guy in the passenger seat. He pointed his gun at Dawn while the hood beside me brought up my own gun. I flinched when the two shots came. Seconds passed before I realized I was somehow still alive — and those muted shots had been made by a gun fitted with a silencer.

Through staring eyes I saw the bruiser in the front seat suddenly jerk and fall clumsily against the car door. The man beside me had fallen back in his seat, his eyes staring upward but seeing nothing. There was a red-purple hole in the middle of his forehead. Blood had spattered the rear window.

Beside me, Dawn opened her mouth to scream. Without thinking, I grabbed her and placed a hand over her mouth. 'Keep quiet, Dawn,' I said in a low voice. 'I don't know what's happening but it seems we have a friend.'

The driver replaced the gun somewhere under the dashboard and then said sharply, 'All right, Merak. Heave these two bodies out and then get back in. Make sure you get your gun back.'

I took the .38 from the dead guy's hand and thrust it into the holster. Then I did as the driver said, watching their bodies drop over the cliff edge before getting back into the car and closing the door behind me. Dawn grabbed my arm and hung on to me as the driver spun the car in a short dizzying circle before straightening up and putting his foot down on the accelerator. I could feel her trembling against me as we raced up the steep incline, passing Florencio's mansion, and then hitting the main highway.

Very soon we were heading towards the town centre. I had no idea where we were being taken. Maybe, I mused, it was someplace where we would be in just as much danger as at Florencio's. I experienced a sharp sense of surprise when the car slid to a stop in front of the block housing my office.

'You can go now.' The driver threw a quick glance at both of us. 'I would suggest that from now on you keep a sharp look out for Florencio. He won't be too pleased when he learns what's happened. It's possible he may decide to come after you again.'

We got out. As I leaned forward to close the rear door, I asked, 'Just who are you working for?'

I didn't really expect an answer — but I got one. 'Enrico Manzelli.'

The next moment the limousine was speeding into the distance. I looked round at Dawn. Her eyes were wide and the frightened look was still there.

Manzelli! That was something I hadn't anticipated.

We went inside. There was a notice pinned to the door of the elevator. It must have been put there while we had been gone. It read: OUT OF ORDER so we had to walk up the four flights before reaching the office.

Here Dawn made the coffee and this time she didn't register disapproval when

I poured a slug of whiskey into mine. Surprisingly, she nodded when I offered the bottle to her.

I took a large swallow even though the coffee burned my mouth and throat. I needed it. The tension slowly drained from me. After a pause I said, 'From what just happened it would seem that Manzelli not only knows everything that goes on in L.A. but he's still the Big Boss.'

'That may be true but I doubt he saved our lives just to prove that to the other outfits. I think he must have some other reason.'

'I think you're right. I reckon he did it because he still needs my help. He figures I'm the only one who can sort out this unholy mess.'

'But why you?'

I finished my drink in a couple of swallows even though it burned my mouth and throat. Then I lit a cigarette. It steadied my nerves a little. 'My guess is that he's afraid some of the outfits are ready to join forces against him. A lot of the bosses don't like being dictated to by him. He needs all the help he can get — even mine.'

Dawn placed her cup down on the table. Her eyes were still wide and she still seemed scared by all that had happened. 'To be quite honest, Johnny, I don't see there's much you can do. There are two dead men, a little guy on the run with over a million dollars of the Organization's money, and Florencio who wants you permanently out of the equation.'

I leaned back and watched a smoke ring ascending slowly towards the ceiling. After a pause, I said, 'You know, Dawn, I have the strange feeling that we're missing something here; something that's been staring us in the face from the very beginning and we just can't see it.'

'You still think that whoever killed that man in Igor Karmov's house is the same one who murdered Sergei?'

'As sure as I can be about anything in this weird case. I'm also fairly sure he's the same one who tried to kill Dexter.'

'But why? As far as I can see there's no connection there.'

Sighing, I sat back and at that moment there came a knock on the door. It was a hesitant sort of knock as if who was there wasn't quite sure they should be. There was a pause and then the door opened. It was certainly the last person I expected to be calling on me — Zelda Marshall!

5

The Rats Go On The Run

Without a word she closed the door quietly behind her, then turned. She was still the same Zelda, elegantly turned out, her make-up to perfection — and yet I noticed something different from the last time I'd seen her. There were dark circles under her eyes and she looked as though she hadn't slept for a week. She also looked scared.

She threw a glance at Dawn who then moved pointedly back to her desk. Something passed between them but that was something between two women and I didn't try to figure out what it was.

'I thought you'd decided to hire another private investigator,' I said. I did my best to keep the note of sarcasm out of my voice. 'So just what are you doing here?'

She made no move to sit down but just

stood there with her hands clasped in front of her. Then she licked her lips, and said quietly, 'I'm sorry I was so rude the last time I came but I desperately need your help. I received another of those death threats this morning. Whoever is sending them I'm sure they mean it.'

'O.K. Sit down and let me see it.'

She sat down on the edge of the chair and then rummaged inside her shoulder bag, bringing out a folded piece of paper. It was similar to the last. This time, however, it said: *Make the most of today. It will be your last.*

Placing the warning on the desk I said, 'Now let me guess. Those other P.I.s you've approached have refused to help you when they found out you were associated with Florencio.'

'Yes.' She was looking down at the floor and the single word was little more than a whisper.

'I thought so.' I looked across at Dawn; saw the almost imperceptible shake of her head. I knew what she was thinking. Turning to Zelda, I continued, 'I can't say I blame them. After our experience of a little while ago, it wouldn't be healthy for any of them.'

A look of incomprehension crossed her face; 'I don't understand. What sort of experience was that?'

'Your boyfriend had a couple of men take us for a drive. I'm sure you get the picture. It was meant to be our last.'

She bit her lower lip. Evidently she knew nothing of this. 'I didn't know. But why would he want to kill you?'

'I think it's pretty obvious. I know too much. The men in the Organization don't like it when anyone starts poking into their affairs. They have a nasty habit of making such people disappear.'

'Then there's nothing you'll do for me?' She was trembling now, her hands shaking.

'There might be one thing I can do.'

'What is it? I'll do anything you ask.'

'Obviously you don't understand how the Underworld works. Someone has hired a professional assassin to kill you. These death threats spell out when you're to die. The usual thing is that you have to be killed at that specific time.

'That's what must happen. If it isn't carried out to the letter then the hit is off and the guy who's supposed to carry it out faces the consequences of his failure. So all we have to do is keep you alive until tomorrow.'

'And how do you propose to do that?' Dawn asked with a trace of acid in her voice.

'There's only one way,' I told her. 'We'll have to keep her in a safe place for the night. At the moment we don't know who's put out this hit on you. It may even be your boyfriend for all I know.'

'Michael would never do a thing like that,' Zelda protested vehemently.

'When you're dealing with the Organization you have to take every possibility into account,' I said. 'You can be sure of nothing.'

'And where do you suggest we let her stay for the night?' This time Dawn's tone was distinctly hostile. 'Your place or mine?'

'Neither. I have an old friend I've known from way back. She owes me a favour and no one will find you there. You weren't followed here, were you?'

Zelda shook her head. 'I'm sure I wasn't.'

'Good.' I glanced at my watch. 'It's getting late. I guess we can close up now. Then I'll take you to Marla's. She was a showgirl in the old days but don't let appearances fool you. If I was to give her the word she'll shoot anyone who tries to get in.'

Forty minutes later we were in Burbank, driving along a quiet road with trees growing along either side. In the old days it had seen its share of violence. Now it just slumbered the days and years away with an air of shabby tranquillity.

The house was in the middle of a row of small buildings, all virtually identical. I knocked, saw one of the curtains move slightly, and then I heard a key turn in the lock. The door opened and Marla stood there, peering at me through thick-lensed spectacles.

The expression of surprised recognition on her face was almost immediate. 'Johnny! My God, how many years has it been?'

'Too many, Marla,' I said. 'May we come in?'

'Of course. Of course.' She stood on one side to allow us to enter. Closing the door behind us, she turned the key in the lock. 'You can't be too careful these days,' she added, glancing inquiringly from Dawn to Zelda.

'Sit down, all of you, if you can find room. I don't usually get many visitors these days.'

Seating herself in a large rocking chair in one corner of the room, she stared directly at me. 'You in some kind of trouble, Johnny?'

'Not me personally,' I came directly to the point. 'My friend here, Zelda, needs a safe place for the night.'

'What's your problem, Zelda?' she asked. 'Is it the cops or the Mobs?'

'Why do you ask that, Marla?' I inquired.

She gave a knowing smile. 'It's usually one or the other where young women are concerned. Unless, of course, you're on the run from a jealous boyfriend.'

'Someone has put out a hit on her.' I

sat back in the old, but very comfortable, armchair.

Marla sucked in her lower lip. 'When is the hit for?'

'Today.' Zelda held out the last threat she'd received. Marla scrutinized it carefully, then nodded. 'I get the picture. You're hoping that if they don't kill you tonight, you might be safe. You got any idea who did this? Obviously someone wants you out of the way.'

Zelda shook her head. 'I can't think of anyone who'd want to kill me.' There was a distinct tremor in her voice. 'Can you help me? Johnny seems to think you can.'

'I've had plenty of experience of these hoodlums in the past. That's why I always keep a gun handy.' She pointed to the far wall. A shotgun rested on a couple of large hooks. 'And I always keep this with me.' Digging down the side of her chair she brought out what I recognized as a Smith and Wesson.

'You know how to use these guns?' Dawn asked, her eyes wide.

'Not only how to use them, dearie, I will use them. Make no mistake about that. I'm also a light sleeper. Believe me, anyone tries to get in here won't walk out again.'

'Then I reckon you'll be in safe hands, Zelda,' I said, getting up. 'I'm pretty certain no one knows you're here. Thanks, Marla. I owe you one.'

'Any time, Johnny. And don't make it so long before you come again.'

'I'll be round tomorrow morning.'

Dawn and I went out to the car. As far as I could see the street was deserted. There were lights showing in a few of the windows but everything appeared normal.

'Are you sure she'll be all right there, Johnny?' Dawn asked as she got into the car.

'She'll be O.K. I've known Marla for a long time. Hard as nails. Like I said, she was in the chorus line in the old days and they spent much of their time fighting off the guys who came in for the shows.'

'I hope you're right. Somehow, I have a funny feeling about all this.'

I put the car into gear and drove away. I wasn't too sure either but I didn't say anything. Those little mice were having a fine old time raising doubts in my mind as to whether I'd done the right thing. The next morning, after Dawn had made the breakfast, we drove back to Marla's place. There was no answer when I knocked twice on the door and that was when I started to get really worried. The door opened as I turned the knob and a quick look told me the lock had been forced.

'You'd better stay out here, Dawn,' I said harshly.

She gave me a worried look; then stepped back. I think she knew what was coming.

Thrusting the door open I stepped inside. The room was in virtual darkness with all of the curtains closed and I snapped on the light.

Marla lay half out of the rocking chair. The gun she kept there was on the floor beside her. Picking it up by the end of the barrel, I checked that it was still loaded and it hadn't been fired. The shotgun was still on the wall. The blood down the front of her dress told me that she must have died almost instantly.

Zelda lay just behind the door. There was blood on her dress too from a shoulder wound. I felt for the pulse. It was weak but steady.

Without getting to my feet, I yelled, 'Get a doctor and an ambulance, Dawn. Zelda is still alive. You'd also better phone the cops.'

The ambulance arrived within ten minutes with a couple of cop cars close behind. As I'd guessed the guys who came in were Lieutenant O'Leary and Sergeant Kolowinski.

O'Leary looked at me and shook his head. 'I'm not even going to ask, Merak,' he said sharply. 'But I guess you're going to tell me just how you happen to be here.'

I indicated Zelda. 'Dawn and I brought this woman here last night because she had a threat telling her she'd be dead before this morning. I figured this would be a safe place for her to stay.'

O'Leary glanced around the room. 'Obviously it wasn't,' he remarked sarcastically. He jerked a thumb towards Marla's body. 'Who's she?'

'A close friend of mine from the old

times,' I told him. 'She agreed to allow this woman to stay here for the night. She — '

A shout from Kolowinski interrupted me. 'There's a gun over here, Lieutenant.' He took a pencil from his pocket, inserted it into the barrel and lifted the weapon, bringing it into the light. 'It's a .22. It would seem to have been fired twice and pretty recently.'

'Is that the same calibre as yours, Merak?' the Lieutenant said pointedly.

'My gun's here,' I pulled open my jacket and showed him the weapon nestling in its holster. 'And as you can see, it's a .38.'

'Bag that gun,' O'Leary said to Kolowinski. 'And send it to ballistics. I don't doubt we'll find it's the murder weapon. Whoever did this must've dropped it when they made their getaway.'

One of the ambulance guys said, 'This woman has a slug in the top of her right shoulder, Lieutenant. We should get her to hospital right away.'

O'Leary ran a hand down his cheek and then gave a terse nod. 'All right. You can take her.' He moved across to where Marla lay slumped in the rocking chair. 'This one is for the morgue. I want this place sealed off and everything searched and dusted for prints although this looks to me like a typical gangland killing. I've no doubt they intended to kill the other woman too. If she makes it, I'll want to talk to her. In the meantime, you'll have to answer some questions, Merak.'

'Somehow, I guessed that was coming.' I still felt pretty shaken by all that had happened. I'd been so sure that this was a safe place. Clearly I was wrong but how the hell had the killer followed us to Marla's?

O'Leary motioned to me to go outside. Dawn was standing there. Her face was. white and strained and she didn't look too good. Evidently this had hit her as hard as it had me.

'You know that dame they've just taken away?' The Lieutenant took out a cigarette and lit it.

'Not very well. She's going about with Michael Florencio, a big man in Malloy's outfit.'

'I know who he is,' O'Leary snapped. 'And just what's your connection with her?'

'She came to me a couple of days ago with a death threat she'd received — wanted me to help her. When I found out she's Florencio's girlfriend and tried to talk about it, she turned nasty and walked out. Dawn can verify that.'

Dawn nodded. 'All of that is perfectly true, Lieutenant.'

'Then late yesterday she turned up again, scared to death, and very apologetic. I figured it was a gangland hit. Maybe you're not familiar as to how these hits work, Lieutenant. Generally, if the killer fails to carry out the hit by the given time, he gets it in the neck instead of the victim.'

'I wasn't aware of that,' the Lieutenant admitted. 'Some kind of honour among killers?'

'You could look at it that way, I guess. Anyway, I knew Marla, the dame who lived here, and she owed me a favour. So Dawn and I brought Zelda here for the night and we arranged to come back for her this morning. When we arrived we discovered the lock had been forced and this is what we found.'

O'Leary stared down at the glowing tip of his cigarette in silence. He was obviously turning over everything I had told him in his mind. Finally, he said, 'So your guess would be that this killer somehow found out your client was here, broke in with the intention of killing this Zelda Marshall?'

'I can't think of anything else at the moment. Everything must've happened within seconds. Marla was a light sleeper and she always had that Smith and Wesson beside her. If she'd had a chance, you can be sure he'd never have got in. I'd say she was shot first since she had the gun.'

O'Leary digested that, still looking puzzled. Then he said, 'I'd be inclined to buy that but for one thing. Once Marla was killed, he'd have plenty of time to carry out the hit and shoot this Zelda woman. I'm assuming she didn't have a gun with her when she came?'

'Not that I know of, Lieutenant.'

'Yet he seemed to have panicked at that moment. She only has a shoulder wound and he also dropped his gun when he fled. Doesn't that seem strange?'

'Maybe he was disturbed and had to get away in a hurry,' Dawn suggested.

'And this Zelda dame. Did she give you any indication as to who might have sent those threats?'

Shaking my head, I said, 'None at all. She claimed she had no idea who it could be.'

'And you, Merak? Do you have any idea who'd want her dead?'

'I could make a few guesses. Since it looks to me like a gang killing I'd say it was someone pretty high up in the outfits who didn't like the idea of her getting cosy with Florencio.'

O'Leary thought that over. Then he tossed his cigarette butt away and said, 'All right, you can both go. Just stick around. There might be other questions I'll have to ask you.'

'I'll be around, Lieutenant.'

'Oh, and one more thing, Merak.'

'Yes, Lieutenant?'

'When the next murder occurs in L.A. please make sure you're not within a hundred miles of it. I'm getting really fed up finding you at every crime scene I'm called to.'

We drove back to the office not saying a word during the whole of the journey. I knew we were both blaming ourselves for what had happened — one person dead and another in hospital possibly critically wounded.

Once inside the office, I slumped down into the chair behind the desk, stretching out my legs. I reached inside the drawer and took out the bottle of Scotch and sat staring at it for a moment.

'Go on, Johnny,' Dawn said watching me closely. 'I think I'll have one too.'

I poured out the two drinks and handed one to her. I drank the Scotch slowly, hoping it would help to clear my head. At the back of my mind, I wondered what Michael Florencio would do once he got all the facts. It wasn't likely he would still believe we were dead.

When that car and his two henchmen failed to return, he'd want to know why.

It wouldn't be long before the real driver was found wherever Manzelli's man had left him. He'd soon put two and two together and, knowing Florencio, he wouldn't make five.

Sitting there, with my drink in my hand, I had the sudden feeling that after what had just happened, things were going to break with a vengeance. It wasn't a nice feeling. I knew that, somehow, I had to find the one guy who had started all of this — Igor Karmov! He was the man with most of the answers.

There was just one big problem. Here, in L.A., there were a million rat holes into which Karmov could vanish. Finding the right one was going to be far from easy. I needed to talk with someone who knew all of these bolt holes and I knew of only one man.

Pete Terrans was a small time crook who ran a small pool hall somewhere along the Strip. In the old days he'd acted as a messenger between the various outfits, living most of the time on the wrong side of the law. At times he'd run foul of the Big Men and on at least one occasion I'd helped get him out of a tight spot.

I finished my drink. Dawn swung her gaze on me and said, 'Have another if you like, Johnny. I don't mind.'

'Thanks but I've just remembered someone I have to see.' I could have kicked myself for not having thought of him before.

'You're not going to get yourself into any more trouble, are you?'

'Not with this guy. He's just small fry as far as the Organization is concerned.'

'Anything you want me to do while you're away?'

'Just stand by the phone. If O'Leary rings, tell him I'm out on a case. That may keep him off my back for a while.'

Pete's poolroom was situated in a little alley off one of the main streets in downtown Burbank. It didn't look much from the outside but then it had no ambitions to be pretentious. The clientele who used it were mostly local bums who went in just to be out of the rain or the hot sun.

There were six pool tables and a bar

along one wall. Five of the tables were occupied. Cigarette smoke hung in a heavy curtain over everything. You might just be able to recognize whom you were playing with through the haze. Pete was standing with another guy behind the bar.

He was wiping glasses and didn't look up until I reached the counter in front of him. Then his eyes widened a little.

Around the cigarette dangling from his lower lip, he said hoarsely, 'Johnny Merak! What the hell brings you to my place?'

'Get me a whiskey, Pete and then I'll tell you,' I said.

He brought a glass and bottle and poured out a shot. Pushing it across the counter, he leaned forward. A length of ash fell from the tip of his cigarette and he wiped it away with his apron.

'I need your help and some information, Pete. I'm looking for a guy who's trying to keep out of sight and I figure you know most, if not all, of the hiding places in L.A.'

'Who's this guy wanted by? The cops or the Big Men?'

'The cops would like to speak to him but as far as I know he's not committed any crime.'

Pete screwed his face up into a scowl. 'That means someone in the Organization wants him.'

'Someone who might just finish him off unless I can get to him first,' I acknowledged.

He thought that over for a minute, his small, deep-set eyes fixed on nothing. Then he straightened.

'Come through into the back room,' he said quietly. 'We can talk there.' He took the bottle from the counter and indicated I was to bring my glass with me.

The room at the rear of the premises was small but less smoky than the poolroom. There was a table and a couple of chairs that looked as if they'd been brought over on the Mayflower.

'Sit down, Johnny, and tell me the name of this guy you're looking for. I may have heard of him.'

I sat down gingerly expecting the chair to collapse beneath my weight. 'His name is Igor Karmov,' I told him.

He paused suddenly, the top of the bottle over his glass. 'Karmov! The guy who took all that dough from Sharky Dexter?'

'The same.'

'You're not working for Dexter, are you?'

'In a way,' I admitted. 'He's hired me to find him and — '

Pete leaned towards me and grasped my arm. 'Listen to me, Johnny.' His voice was little more than a throaty whisper. 'Sharky Dexter is a bad guy to get mixed up with. I'd say that with all the men he has, he could find this guy Karmov whenever he wants to. Take my advice and get out of this case as quickly as you can.'

'I'm afraid there's no way I can do that, Pete. Now — can you help me or not?'

'All right. On your own head be it.' He sighed and leaned back. 'Karmov would need help if he was to stay out of sight of the Organization. And it would have to be someone who has no respect or liking for the Mobs.'

'Do you know anyone who would fit the bill?'

'I reckon there's only one man. He wouldn't do it for peanuts but since Karmov has over a million bucks, he might help him stay hidden.'

'And get safely out of the country?'

'That may be possible too.'

'So who is this guy, Pete, and where can I find him?'

'His name's Carlos Donetti. But you won't be able to find or contact him. I may be able to get word to him but whether he'll get in touch with you is entirely up to him. As you can imagine, he's a very cautious guy. In the past he's got several people out of the country, people the Mobs want.'

'This is urgent, Pete. See what you can do.'

'All right. I'll try. If I'm successful, he'll make his own decision. If he decides to help you find Igor Karmov, he'll be in touch within the next few days. That's all I can do, I'm afraid.'

'Thanks a lot, Pete. I won't forget this.'

6

The Lady Disappears

The next day I got a visit from Lieutenant O'Leary. It was early in the afternoon and I was sitting at my desk just finishing my lunch. Dawn was spending the afternoon at her own place since there wasn't much for her to do at the moment. Tossing the paper bag that had contained my sandwiches into the wastepaper basket, I was just lighting a cigarette when he came in. This time he knocked before pushing the door open.

'You got a few minutes, Merak?' he asked, sitting down and placing his hat on the desk. I shrugged. It wasn't often he asked it as politely as that. Clearly there was something worrying him.

'Sure. I've got all the time in the world for you, Lieutenant.'

He didn't know whether or not I was being sarcastic but he let it pass. 'That murder of your friend,' he began. 'There are quite a few things about it that stick in my craw.'

'Such as?'

'Firstly there were no prints on that .22 we found in the room. So either our killer wore gloves or he wiped it clean.'

'Then you've got to accept that he wore gloves,' I said.

His brows went up. 'What makes you so damned sure?'

Shrugging, I said, 'If he didn't he wouldn't stop to wipe it clean of prints and then drop it on the way out — unless he meant to leave it there for you to find.'

O'Leary considered that and then shook his head emphatically. 'But that doesn't make any sense either. Why would he do that? These killers are professionals. They aren't usually so obliging.'

I stubbed out my cigarette and lit another. This case was getting weirder by the minute. 'What else is worrying you, Lieutenant?' I asked.

He scratched his chin. 'How much do you know about this dame we found

— Zelda Marshall?'

'Not much. Word has it that she's Michael Florencio's girlfriend. She arrived in L.A. some years ago with almost no money to her name. Within nine months she had this big chain of boutiques. I guess you can put two and two together and reach your own conclusion. Why do you ask? You reckon she's somehow involved?'

'I've no idea where she fits into all this. All I know is that she discharged herself from the hospital some time during the night and now she's vanished.'

I sat up straight at that. It was the last thing I'd expected. 'But I thought she'd been seriously wounded. When I found her I reckoned she'd still be fighting for her life.'

'Well it seems she only had a flesh wound in the right shoulder. The slug must have just grazed her. The doctor wanted to keep her under observation for another couple of days but she refused. I've now got an APB out on her. There are a lot of questions I want answered.'

'Not as many as me,' I said. 'And as for

Zelda, I reckon I know where I'll find her.'

'Where?' He snapped the word.

'Somehow, I don't think you'd be welcome there, Lieutenant. Unless I miss my guess she's gone running back to Florencio.'

'You're not thinking of going there, are you?'

'He's already tried to get rid of me once. Somehow I don't think he'll make the same mistake again. This time I have a guardian angel and I figure Florencio has already received his orders.'

I thought O'Leary was too dumb to know what I was talking about but he did. 'Are you still working hand in hand with Manzelli?'

'I sometimes do little things for him,' I admitted.

'All of which are probably illegal.' He picked up his hat and jammed it onto his head. 'I'll pretend I didn't hear what you just said but remember this. Step over the line in anything you do for that crook, and I'll have you arrested and your licence revoked. I'll make damned sure you never work in this state again.'

He left and I sat there trying to figure out the best way to approach Florencio. I knew O'Leary never made idle threats. I opened the desk drawer and looked at the almost empty bottle of Scotch, then shut the drawer again.

I didn't know how much more of this hell I was going to raise before I was finished with this mess. But whatever was going to happen, I needed a clear head to think things through. I needed to know more about Zelda Marshall. Why she had discharged herself from hospital and what she was doing now.

She obviously knew what she was letting herself in for when she had joined up with Florencio. Somehow, I didn't think she was scared of the guy. She'd have known the type he was — a womaniser who had used a string of women for his own ends and might soon finish with her. If she thought she was the woman who could tame him and keep him on the straight and narrow, she was deluding herself.

Those little mice were still running

around inside my head when Dawn arrived.

'You look more worried than ever, Johnny,' she said by way of greeting. 'Has something happened?'

'O'Leary has only just left,' I told her. 'He came to tell me that Zelda has vanished. Besides I figured you were taking the afternoon off.'

She ignored my last remark. Her neatly curved eyebrows went up at the information about Zelda. 'You mean someone has taken her from the hospital?'

'Not taken. She apparently left of her own free will.'

'But how could she? When they took her from that house I wouldn't have given much for her chances.'

'It seems that .22 slug just grazed her right shoulder. The doctors wanted her to stay in hospital for observation for another couple of days. But she insisted on discharging herself. There was nothing they could do but let her go.'

I meant to say something more but at that moment the phone rang. I recognized Jack Kolowinski's voice. 'Is the

Lieutenant still there, Johnny?'

'No, he left just a few minutes ago. Why, is it something urgent?'

There was quite a long pause; then he came on again. 'I don't know whether I should be telling you this, Johnny. But I guess it'll be all over the front pages in this evening's newspapers.'

'Go on. Spill it,' I said, wondering what was coming next.

'Michael Florencio's dead. It's only just happened.'

I jerked upright in my chair, completely stunned by what I'd just heard.

'Are you still there, Johnny?'

Somehow, I managed to say, 'Yeah, I'm still here. You're absolutely sure about this? How the hell did it happen?'

'I don't have many details yet but it would seem that someone got at him through the window using a high-powered rifle.' A short pause, then, 'Remember, you haven't heard any of this from me, Johnny.'

'Of course not, but — ' The phone suddenly went dead. I guessed that Lieutenant O'Leary had walked into the room at that moment.

Replacing the receiver, I sat back. Dawn was looking at me with an inquiring expression on her face.

'I guess I'll have to forget any plans of going to talk with Florencio,' I said.

Her expression of relief was immediately replaced by one of puzzlement. 'Why — what's happened?'

'That was Jack Kolowinski looking for Lieutenant O'Leary. It would seem that someone using a high-powered rifle has just put paid to Michael Florencio.'

'He's dead?'

Nodding, I said, 'I guess that puts an end to my main theory. So far, I've gone on the assumption that all of these killings have been carried out by the same person. Now, with Florencio dead, that doesn't figure. He doesn't seem to fit into the picture at all.'

'So what's left?'

'I'd say this is a one-off killing. And are you thinking about the same person as I am?'

'Zelda Marshall?'

'It seems more than coincidental he

159

should be shot just after she got herself out of hospital.'

I realized I was drumming on the desktop with my fingers. Zelda had certainly jumped into my mind. But what possible motive could she have for killing him? I'd no proof that he'd pushed her aside for another woman — and it would have taken an expert shot to kill him from a distance through the window.

Zelda had struck me as the kind of woman who knew on which side her bread was buttered. I didn't think she would kill the goose that laid the golden eggs unless she had a very good reason.

There was, of course, another candidate for the killer. Manzelli! He'd already shown that he had no liking for Florencio by the way he'd rescued Dawn and I. If he'd given the order to eliminate Florencio then my guess was that O'Leary would never find the real killer. Manzelli always made sure there were no loose ends lying around that could tie him in with any killing.

Pushing back my chair, I said, 'I think I'll take a drive out to Florencio's place anyway and see if I can find anything.'

'Do you think that would be wise, Johnny? Kolowinski gave you that information in confidence. If you suddenly turn up on the scene, O'Leary will know who told you.'

'Not if he doesn't see me. There's a pair of binoculars around somewhere. I'll need them.'

Dawn rummaged inside one of the drawers of her desk and brought them out. 'I'm coming with you, Johnny,' she said firmly. 'Whenever you go out alone you always seem to land in trouble of some kind.'

It was useless to argue with her. Once her mind was made up it remained as solid as the Rock of Gibraltar.

Just over half an hour later we were approaching the narrow road leading up to Florencio's place. I stopped the car in a small lay-by, out of sight from the house and screened from the road by a row of thick vegetation. I got out. The area around us was covered with dense bushes that enabled us to pull ourselves up the slope until we were almost on the same level as the building.

A couple of police cars were parked outside and as we watched a uniformed office came out and walked over to one of them. He got inside without closing the door. He seemed to be talking to someone on the car's intercom.

Switching my attention from him, I mentally calculated which of the windows was that in Florencio's office where we'd been previously taken. Through the binoculars it was just possible to make out the neat round hole in the glass pane. I could also see the shapes of several people inside the room.

Lowering the binoculars I handed them to Dawn. 'It's the third window to the left of the door. If you look closely you can just make out the bullet hole in the glass.'

'So the shot must've come from this direction,' she murmured, adjusting the focus slightly.

'That doesn't surprise me. There's plenty of cover here and a clear view of his office. Whoever killed him must have known something about the layout of the house and his normal routine; knew he'd be in there at that particular time.'

I threw a swift glance around me. 'It wouldn't be difficult to get away without being spotted. Have a car waiting at the bottom of the slope and there would be a quick getaway.'

I took back the binoculars and scanned the rest of the building. There was not much police activity outside and I guessed O'Leary was one of the blurred figures I could see through the punctured window.

'Do you think they've already searched this area, Johnny?' Dawn asked suddenly.

'It doesn't take the intelligence of an Archbishop to figure out the killer was standing somewhere around here when the shot was fired,' I replied. 'I reckon O'Leary would have had a couple of men scouring this place as soon as they discovered what had happened.'

'So there won't be much left for us to find?'

'The Lieutenant is usually pretty thorough.'

Dawn edged sideways through the bushes, staring down at the ground at her feet. I didn't think she'd discover anything. But a few moments later she bent and picked up something.

'What is it?' I asked, going up to her.

She held it out to me. It was a small jewelled hairpin.

'Now that's a strange thing to find here,' I remarked. 'We've no absolute proof it belongs to the killer but if it does, it certainly narrows the number of suspects down a little.'

'I'd say it's beginning to point to Zelda,' Dawn replied.

'You could be right. But O'Leary will want motive, means and opportunity. As far as we know at the moment, all Zelda has is opportunity. She could easily have left the hospital and got here in time to shoot Florencio.

'But where does a woman like her pick up a high-powered rifle? And what motive does she have for killing him? No, Dawn, I reckon we'll have to dig a little deeper for the answer to this one.'

She gave me an enigmatic look. 'You still believe that all of these murders are tied together and were carried out by the same person?'

'It's just a gut feel I've got — nothing

more.' I looked back towards the house. There was a lot more activity going on now. Two guys wheeled the body out on a trolley and it was put into the back of a waiting ambulance. O'Leary appeared. He was giving orders to a couple of cops who then went off and began stringing tape around the place, sealing it off as a crime scene.

'I think we'd better make ourselves scarce,' I said. 'I wouldn't like O'Leary to spot the car down there.'

Dawn nodded and quickly followed me down the slope. Less than five minutes later we were on the main highway and heading back into town.

Once inside the office I switched on the light. It was now getting dark and almost closing up time.

'Are you hungry?' I asked. 'I know a nice little Italian restaurant just around the corner if you care for something to eat.'

'I'd like that.' She smiled. 'It'll feel good to get away from this case, even if only for an hour or so.'

I knew she was thinking more about

me than herself when she said that.

We found a table near the window. I'd always figured Eugene, the proprietor, for the romantic Italian type. The place was lit entirely by candles placed on each table. I'd known Eugene for quite a number of years but this was the first time I'd been there with Dawn. He gave her an appraising look then glanced at me with an almost imperceptible nod of approval.

Once we had ordered, I sat back and surveyed the other customers. There weren't many at that early hour. Come eleven o'clock and the restaurant would be crowded. A young couple sat at the table nearest the door and there was a guy sitting alone at one of the other tables.

He didn't seem to be taking any notice of anyone around him but I immediately focused my attention on him. I reckoned he was in his mid-fifties with iron-grey hair and a hard angular face. I had him figured for an ex-ball player or perhaps a professional wrestler.

Dawn leaned forward over the table.

'You seem to be interested in that man over there, Johnny. Do you know him?'

I shook my head. 'I've never seen the guy before but there's something about him that makes me nervous.'

She grabbed my hand and squeezed it tightly. 'We're here to forget all about this case for a little while. Now let's eat.'

As things turned out, even in Eugene's romantic Italian restaurant, the case didn't intend to let us go. We'd just finished the last course and Eugene had brought the wine. Once he'd moved away the big guy at the nearby table got up and tossed several bills onto his plate. I figured he was leaving but suddenly he turned and sat down at our table, easing his bulk into a chair.

'Hey!' I said sharply. My right hand reached instinctively for the .38. 'What do you think you're — ?'

He cut me off, placing a finger to his lips. Softly, he said, 'Pardon this intrusion, Mister Merak, but my time is valuable and since you have asked to see me, I think we should get down to business right away.'

'I've asked to see you?'

'So I understand. My name is Carlos Donetti. My friend Peter Terrans thinks I may be able to help you in some way.'

For a moment, the name didn't click. Then I remembered. Pete Terrans had promised to try to get in touch with this guy to help me find Igor Karmov. Evidently he'd kept his word.

'You certainly can. That is if you agree to help.'

'What is it you want, Mister Merak?'

'I need to find Igor Karmov — and quickly. So far, there've been several murders and if I'm to prevent any more, I must talk to him.'

'I see.' He hunched his shoulders forward and threw a quick glance around the room. Then, evidently satisfied, he went on, 'You understand the nature of my business. I help people to get out of the country. They are people who are wanted by either the police or the various criminal organizations. As you can imagine, this can be a dangerous business and I must be quite sure of everyone I deal with.'

'I understand.'

'Ah, but what you don't understand is that I know you have accepted five thousand dollars from Sharky Dexter to find and turn Karmov over to him.'

'That's true. But that was before all of these people were being killed and it all seems to have started with Karmov winning all that dough.'

Donetti commenced to tap the table with his fingers, beating out a rapid tattoo. He seemed to be finding it difficult to make up his mind. Finally, he said, 'Very well, Mister Merak. I'll take a chance on you but I warn you, double-cross me and you'll find I can be even worse than any of your old associates in the Organization.'

He moved back his chair and got up. 'I believe your office is not far from here and this restaurant would seem a safe place to meet. I'll be here at precisely nine o'clock tomorrow morning. Then I will take you to see Igor Karmov.'

'I'll be here,' I said.

After he had gone, Dawn said softly, 'Can you trust that man, Johnny? After all, you know absolutely nothing about him. This may be a trap.'

'Unfortunately there's nothing else I can do. I'll just have to go along with him. And this time, I'm going alone.'

'But — '

'That's the way it is, Dawn. Besides, I'll need you in the office to head off O'Leary. After Florencio's death, I'm sure he'll be around looking for me.'

7

A Date With Mystery

The next morning I gave Dawn the key to the office and walked slowly around the block. There I stopped. It was just after eight-thirty and from where I was standing I had a clear view of the restaurant.

I knew Eugene opened at nine o'clock on the dot as regularly as clockwork. At that early hour there would be few, if any, customers. Leaning my shoulders against the wall, I lit a cigarette and watched the smoke drift lazily along the street. There had been fog during the latter part of the night. It still clung around most of the buildings but it was thinning quickly now. Several cars went past but none of them stopped near Eugene's.

It wanted five minutes to nine when I spotted the car driving slowly along the opposite side of the street. This time it stopped outside Eugene's and Donetti got out. As far as I could tell, he was alone.

Without a sideways glance, he walked up to the door and rapped loudly on the glass panel. Eugene opened it a moment later and Donetti went inside, closing the door behind him.

Tossing the cigarette butt onto the sidewalk, I moved quickly across the street, opened the door and slipped inside. The place was in semi-darkness with a couple of candles burning on two of the tables. Evidently, I thought, Eugene didn't believe in electricity or he considered candlelight to be more to his Italian taste for the romantic.

Donetti was seated at one of the tables. He glanced at his watch as I walked over. 'I see you are a punctual man, Mister Merak,' he observed. 'I like that in a man.'

'I always try to be on time for anything important,' I told him, sitting down. I came straight to the point. 'You say you can take me to see Igor Karmov?'

'That is correct. I've spoken to

Karmov. At first, he was extremely reluctant to speak to you but I finally persuaded him to do so. Now, if you're ready I will take you to him.'

'I'm ready.'

Eugene opened the door and we went outside to Donetti's car. Getting in, I settled myself into the seat as he turned the key in the ignition and we pulled away from the sidewalk. Soon we hit the freeway and were heading out of town.

There was quite a lot of traffic at that hour of the morning but Donetti was evidently used to it, weaving in and out of the lanes. I noticed, however, that he kept glancing in the rear mirror.

'You think we're being followed?' I asked.

'It has happened before,' he remarked without turning his head. The possibility didn't seem to worry him. 'The Mobs are not complete fools. Some of them suspect what I am doing but so far I've managed to throw them off the scent.'

About ten miles further on, we turned off the main highway and headed south. Here there was very little traffic and even fewer signs of human habitation. It seemed we were entering a wild stretch of wilderness. A range of high hills showed along the horizon ahead of us and it was soon apparent that Donetti was heading straight for them.

'Not much further to go now,' he remarked casually. He suddenly stopped the car. 'Now I'm afraid you must put on this blindfold. Just a precaution, you understand.'

I took the blindfold and put it on, wondering where the hell he was taking me.

He started the car again and soon we were driving over bumpy, uneven ground. I could see nothing but I guessed we'd turned off the broad track and were cutting across open country. There was the occasional swish of tall grass brushing the sides of the car.

I could feel the heat of the sun on my face and attempted to judge its direction from that, finally estimating that we were still heading in a southerly direction. At last we came to a halt.

Donetti said, 'You may remove the

blindfold now, Mister Merak.'

I did so, blinking in the harsh glare. In front of me was the last thing I expected to see. We were on the edge of a large concrete area surrounded on all sides by high hills. Four large helicopters stood in front of two wide hangars. There were a number of other buildings scattered around the perimeter and several men, wearing dark overalls, were visible on the ground.

'My own private airport,' Donetti said with a note of pride in his voice. 'Very few people indeed even know of its existence.'

I whistled thinly through my teeth. 'So this is how you get people out of the country without anyone being aware of it.'

'Exactly. You may not realize it but this is one of the shortest air routes to South America.'

'And Karmov is hidden here?'

He nodded. 'You must understand that he is a very frightened man and it was only with difficulty that I persuaded him to see you.'

'But it's over a week since he took all

that money. Why haven't you shipped him out yet?'

'The answer is quite simple, my friend. He has to be provided with papers. Certain arrangements have also to be made in whichever country he desires to live. Unfortunately all of that takes time.

'I'm sure you understand that the tentacles of the Organization are spread far and wide. The slightest whisper of what I am doing and not only myself, but all those working for me, would be eliminated.'

We got out of the car and Donetti led me towards a small building on the edge of the airport. Opening the door, he ushered me inside. There was a large room, austerely furnished but everything was of the best. A plush blue carpet covered the floor. There was a mahogany table with several chairs and a drinks cabinet in one corner.

Everything a guy could desire while he waited to be shipped out of the country. And in a chair near the window sat a little guy I knew had to be Igor Karmov — the one who had somehow started this twisted trail of murder.

He didn't get up as I approached but sat staring at me with haunted eyes, wondering who I was and what I wanted with him. I sat down in the chair opposite him.

'They tell me that you wish to see me on some urgent matter.'

Apart from Donetti, I didn't know who 'they' were but I nodded. 'My name's Merak. I'm a private investigator,' I said. 'It seems a lot of people, particularly Sharky Dexter, are after your hide.'

I saw a quick, startled look come into his eyes and he flicked a glance in Donetti's direction.

'It's all right,' I hastened to assure him. 'I'm not here to hand you over to Dexter or the cops. That was quite a stunt you pulled in Dexter's that night. How did you do it?'

Instead of answering, he said, 'Perhaps you would like a drink, Mister Merak. It's a thirsty drive all the way from L.A.'

I decided to humour him. 'It's a little early in the day — but why not?'

He poured some into a glass and

pushed it towards me. For an old guy he seemed very alert. Sipping his drink, he said, 'There are several things I cannot tell you. If I were to do so it could lead to disastrous consequences for many people.'

'You know of course that your brother's dead; that he was murdered. There was also one of Malloy's hoodlums killed at your house. And only yesterday, Michael Florencio was shot.'

For some reason that last piece of information shook him. He jerked back in his chair, almost spilling his drink. 'Florencio dead?' He whispered the words as if finding it impossible to believe them.

'The cops seem to think it was his girlfriend, Zelda Marshall, but I'm not so sure.'

'But why kill him? He had nothing to do with this.'

'If you'd only tell me exactly what happened that night at Dexter's casino I might be able to find out.'

He twisted uncomfortably in his chair, finished his drink, and placed it on the table beside him. 'I'm afraid I can't do that. That is something I'll keep locked away in here.' He tapped the side of his head meaningfully.

I switched tactics. 'Do you know a woman named Zelda Marshall?'

He stared down at the drink in his hand, swirling it idly around inside the glass. 'Zelda Marshall. The name's familiar but I can't remember where — ' He broke off abruptly, then continued, 'Ah, yes. She has a number of stores in L.A. That must have been where I've seen the name. I'm afraid I know nothing else about her. Why do you ask?'

'Nothing really.' It was obvious he was telling the truth.

Donetti stepped forward. 'Is there anything more you want to ask of him?'

I turned back to Karmov. 'Did you kill that man in your house — or your brother?'

He shook his head vehemently. 'No.'

Strangely, I believed him. But there was one more question I had to ask. 'Did you have any part at all in their deaths, or the attempt on Dexter's life?'

He hesitated at that. Then he shook his head. 'No,' he said again.

This time, I had the strange feeling he was lying. I knew if I tried to persist in this line of questioning he would simply clam up on me. I got up.

'Well, thank you for speaking to me. I hope you do get away from the Mobs but even with your friend here to help you, I somehow think you're deluding yourself. Your best chance would be to turn yourself over to the police or the FBI but I know you won't do that. You're absolutely sure you won't tell me how you pulled that stunt at Dexter's?'

I knew from the look on his face that he would never breathe a word of it to anyone.

'Then if there are any more deaths, I hope you can live with your conscience.'

Once we were outside and in the car, Donetti made me put on the blindfold again. He was certainly taking no chance on me finding this place again. We drove back to my office with very few words passing between us. Inwardly, I wondered what made my companion do all of this, getting people out of the clutches of the Organization. I decided he was either a

180

very brave man or a fool.

As I got out of the car in front of the office block, he said quietly, 'Goodbye. Mister Merak. Somehow, I don't think we'll meet again.'

He drove off with a final wave of his hand.

Dawn was there with a look of mute inquiry on her face as I went inside. 'Well?' she asked. 'Did you get to see this Igor Karmov?'

'Donetti kept his word. I saw him. He's hidden away at some private airport way out in the wilds. It seems that Donetti makes a business of getting folk out of the hands of the Mobs. Apparently he's been successful so far but I wouldn't bet a dime on it lasting for long. The Big Boys know it's happening but as yet they haven't found him.' I sat down. 'Anything been happening while I was away?'

She nodded. 'Just as you figured, O'Leary called. I told him you were out and I didn't know when you'd be back.'

At that very moment, the phone shrilled. I didn't have to guess who it was. Lieutenant Shaun O'Leary.

'Where the hell have you been, Merak?' he snarled.

'Out,' I said and that made him even angrier.

'I know you've been out. You left in a car with some guy about two hours ago and you've just arrived back.'

'Now how would you know that, Lieutenant?' I said calmly. 'Unless you've been keeping a tail on me.'

'That's right, I have. Because everywhere you go someone else gets murdered.'

'You seem to have me tagged as the Grim Reaper,' I said. 'Can I help it if folk get bumped off just when I'm around? Anyway, What's on your mind this time?'

'Florencio's dead. Shot by someone outside using a rifle.'

I tried to sound surprised. I didn't want to get Jack Kolowinski into trouble. 'When did this happen?'

'Yesterday. I was surprised not to find you there when I arrived.'

'One can't be in two places at once,' I said and this time I let some of the sarcasm show through.

'Do you know anything about this

dame Florencio was seeing?'

'Very little, I'm afraid. I know she got in with him not long after she arrived in L.A. from somewhere back East. Now, I guess, she's one of the wealthiest women in the state.'

'You think she's the type to commit murder?'

It was a blunt question and I knew he expected an answer. 'Depending on the circumstances, anyone could commit murder.' I knew where this was leading and I didn't want to be drawn into making any statements I might regret later. 'But I get the feeling you've already made up your mind about her. Do you intend to charge her with first-degree murder?'

'Too damned right I do. When I can find her.'

'Have you checked at Florencio's place?'

'I've had men checking everywhere but there's no sign of her. Do you have any ideas?'

'If she's not at that mansion on the seafront, I've no ideas at all.'

He put the phone down. I didn't know whether he believed me but at that moment I didn't care.

Dawn looked at me with a resigned expression. 'If you want my opinion, Johnny, you've reached a dead end. What have you got to go on? A little guy milks Dexter for a million bucks. Then his brother contacts you, gives you Igor's address where one of Malloy's men is killed. Next Igor's brother is murdered and his body fished out of the lake in the park.'

She ticked everything off on her fingers. 'But it doesn't stop there. Dexter nearly dies in a burning office, you get beaten up by Manzelli's gorillas and meet up, quite coincidentally, with this Zelda Marshall who happens to be Michael Florencio's girlfriend. Then we get picked up by Florencio's hired killers and only escape with Manzelli's help. Good God, Johnny! Do I have to go on? This case has turned into a nightmare and you're still no nearer to finding out who the real killer is.'

As always, she was right. There was no

light at the end of the tunnel. Somewhere along it, it was blocked by something I couldn't see even though it was probably staring me in the face. I believed in logic, cause and effect. The trouble was, the effects were all too obvious in the form of dead bodies — it was the cause I couldn't figure out.

Someone was out there, in the shadows, manipulating everything and whatever the plan was — it was something really big. Maybe, I thought, I was treating this case as a string of unconnected killings. The jigsaw was still in pieces and no picture was emerging.

Why had Karmov refused to tell me how he pulled off that trick? After all, he'd got away with it, had enough dough to last him for the few remaining years he had, and with luck he would get to his chosen destination. It would have been no skin off his nose to let me in on it.

Yet the more I thought about it, it hadn't been because it was some secret he didn't want to disclose to anyone else. It wasn't as if he was a magician who had performed a new and baffling trick and was challenging any others in the profession to work it out. He had seemed afraid to tell.

I let my mind wander off at a tangent. So whom was he scared of? Sharky Dexter? Somehow, I didn't think so. Manzelli? I rejected that possibility almost at once. His brother had worked in the Organization but not Igor. I doubted if he even knew about Manzelli.

I finally gave it up. All of the individual elements in the case simply refused to come together to give even a glimmer of what was really happening. I knew Dawn was watching me closely. Maybe she felt just as puzzled as I did.

'I reckon I'll take a walk to clear my head,' I said. 'At the moment my mind is so full of things that don't make sense that I'm going nowhere.'

'Do you mind if I come with you?' she asked.

'Not at all. I may be able to think better if you're with me.'

It was quite pleasant in the mid-afternoon sunlight. At this time of the day there were plenty of people on the sidewalks. Dawn put her arm through mine as we walked through the bustling crowds. For a little while, the case was forgotten.

I didn't want to think of anything, just to give my mind a rest and enjoy the afternoon. But there was always one little bit of me that seemed to be on the alert for anything suspicious. It was something I'd learned in the old days when a bullet might be waiting for you around every corner. That was why the sudden appearance of the car at the far end of the street immediately caught my attention.

There was nothing about the car itself that made it anything out of the ordinary.

Perhaps it was the abruptness of its appearance and the speed it was travelling that made me act instinctively. Or maybe it was that primal instinct from the old days of the Mobs.

Whatever it was, it made me yell a sudden loud warning, grab Dawn around the waist and push her onto her knees against the nearby wall. She uttered a little scream but that was drowned out by the sharp gunshots that came a few seconds later as the car drew alongside where we had been standing a few seconds earlier. I heard the wicked hum of the bullets close to my head as I crouched down, making myself as small as possible.

It was all over in ten seconds.

Getting to my feet, I pulled Dawn upright. Every bit of the colour seemed to have drained from her face and she was shaking violently as she clutched my arm tightly.

'God, Johnny.' Somehow she got the words out. 'Was that intended for us?'

'I doubt if those slugs were meant for anyone else.'

'Did you see who was driving the car?' There was a slight tremor in her voice but she had quickly pulled herself together. She was that kind of woman. No hysterics or anything like that.

'I'm afraid not. Whoever it was they were wearing some kind of hooded coat.'

Somewhere a woman was screaming in a high-pitched voice. I looked around and saw that although Dawn and I had been lucky, a couple of pedestrians hadn't been so fortunate.

A guy was lying on the sidewalk near the wall. One glance told me he'd collected a slug in the arm. A woman a short distance away was clutching her shoulder and there was blood on her dress.

The wail of a police siren interrupted anything more I wanted to say. The patrol car slid to the sidewalk a few moments later and a couple of uniformed cops got out.

I didn't recognize either of them but one seemed to know me for he walked straight up to me. 'What happened here?' he demanded harshly.

A woman in the crowd started talking rapidly in a high-pitched voice but the cop took no notice of her beyond telling his pal to shut her up while he took statements

'Somebody tried to kill us, officer,' I said as calmly as I could.

'How do you know it was you he was aiming at?' inquired the second cop. 'You don't appear to be hurt. Maybe it was those two down there he was aiming at.' He inclined his head towards the two injured folk on the ground.

I took out my wallet and handed him my business card. He scrutinized it carefully and then handed it back. 'A private investigator. So who is it you're investigating? If you were the target then evidently whoever was in that car wanted you out of the way. So my guess is that you're somehow mixed up with the wrong people.'

'You could say that some of them aren't very polite in the way they go about things,' I said.

'Meaning the Mobs?'

'I didn't say that.'

The first cop who had been moving the crowd back a little way came over. To his companion, he said, 'The ambulance will be here in a couple of minutes and we can get these two injured people to hospital. Also a couple of these folk are willing to give statements. As for these two I reckon they should come to the station to give a statement to the Lieutenant.'

'If it's Lieutenant O'Leary he'll vouch for everything I've just told you.'

The cop's eyebrows went up a shade.

'You know the Lieutenant?'

'I've helped him out with a number of cases in the past,' I told him.

'Then I reckon you've got nothing to worry about.'

They put us in the back of the patrol car and a moment later one of the cops was driving us away from the scene. With the siren going, the drive to the precinct took only five minutes.

O'Leary was seated in his office with Sergeant Kolowinski when we got there. He didn't look too pleased when he saw me. In fact he looked downright angry.

'What is it this time?' he demanded. 'Everywhere I turn, you seem to be there. Can't you ever keep out of trouble, Merak?'

I spread my hands. 'May we sit down, Lieutenant?'

He reluctantly waved his hand towards a couple of chairs. Placing the tips of his fingers together, he looked from Dawn to me, a frown on his face. 'What happened?' He repeated his earlier question.

'Dawn and I had just decided to take a walk along Wiltshire when this car came screaming around the corner, heading straight for us. I guess some instinct told me they weren't late for some party so I grabbed Dawn and pushed her to the ground just before the place was sprayed with bullets.'

'You were just enjoying a walk along Wiltshire when someone tried to kill you.' There was a distinct note of disbelief in the Lieutenant's voice. 'I can understand quite a lot of people wanting you dead, Merak. I feel that way myself at times. But you expect me to believe that some mind-reader knew you'd be in that exact place at that time if, as you say, you'd just decided to take a walk?'

Shrugging, I said, 'It's quite possible that, whoever it was, is a very patient person, Lieutenant. They could have been watching my office in case we did go out sometime and followed us to Wiltshire.'

'Possible, but hardly likely. I don't suppose you got the registration of the car or any description of the driver?'

'Sorry — no. Everything happened so fast that all I thought about was getting my head down.'

'All right, Merak. I'll check with any witnesses and see if they can add anything further. You'll be only too aware that very few folk want to be involved in shootings like this. In the meantime just get on with whatever cases you have and leave me to do my job. I've got enough on my plate without worrying about you.'

He looked down at the sheaf of papers on his desk and motioned to Kolowinski to see us out. The meeting was over as far as he was concerned.

'Do you reckon he'll do anything?' Dawn asked as we got outside.

'Somehow, I doubt it. He knows there's virtually no chance of picking up whoever was driving that car. He won't waste time running around in circles. My guess is that any statements he gets from Joe Public will be filed away and forgotten.'

There seemed little point in going back to the office now. I'd reached the end of all the leads I had and come up with nothing.

Dawn made something to eat and we sat at the table, sitting mostly in silence. I still had the hunch that something was staring me in the face but I couldn't recognize it. I felt sure there was a single thread tying all of these incidents together but I was damned if I could figure out what it was.

Dawn put away the dishes and came back. She looked unusually thoughtful. As she sat down again she said, 'Are you still trying to figure out how Karmov managed to beat the roulette table, Johnny?'

'Yes — and getting nowhere. With the setup Dexter has beneath those tables, anyone running them can make that ball drop into any number they like, and — '

I stopped abruptly because it was at that moment that the answer hit me right between the eyes. 'Of course. That was how it was done. It's so simple that I overlooked it completely. There's only one possible way the ball came up on number thirteen three times in succession.'

'Oh, and what might that be?'

'That little guy didn't work any magic. He just did exactly as he'd been told. He put the money on number thirteen and

Dexter did the rest! If they were in it together it would be easy for Dexter to manipulate that magnetic set-up under that table and then make sure that the ball always fell into number thirteen and — '

'So that's how it was done.' Dawn nodded. 'I think you're right, that's the only way it could have happened.'

I ran the idea through my mind. It certainly seemed to make perfect sense. Then another thought struck me. 'But why would Dexter part with all that money to someone like Karmov who's probably never played roulette before in his life?'

She looked a little disappointed; then went on. 'Whatever it was, there must have been a very good reason for it, something worth a million dollars.'

I felt sure she was right. But there were still a lot of questions remaining unanswered. Had it been part of the plan for Karmov to disappear with the dough?

There'd been no doubt in my mind that the little guy was sufficiently scared to want to get out of the country. So if

Dexter wasn't after him — who was?

There was also another big question mark hanging over everything. Dexter had not only convinced me that he wanted Karmov and his money back — but why had he involved me at all if he'd deliberately worked with Karmov to lose all that money?

Commonsense told me that I was right about the way it had been done. But that threw up more questions that didn't make sense. I decided to let things simmer for a while to see if my mind popped up with anything more. A few more pieces of the jigsaw had now been fitted together but it didn't seem to be tied in with anything else.

There was still no clear picture emerging.

8

The Lady Returns

I spent the next couple of days trying to figure out the various ramifications of the idea that Dexter and Karmov had fixed the roulette scam together. My mind told me it was the only logical explanation. Yet it didn't explain what had subsequently happened.

Where did Sergei Karmov fit in and why had he been murdered? Who had tried to kill Dexter? Had it been the same person who had sent the death threats to Zelda Marshall that had resulted in Marla being killed and Zelda shot in the shoulder?

The second morning I arrived late at the office. I'd been up more than half of the night trying to figure everything out. Now I had a blinding headache just behind the temples. Dawn got me a couple of painkillers and made me a cup of hot, black coffee.

'Maybe it would be better if you slowed down a bit, Johnny,' she said over her shoulder as she went back to her desk. 'You're standing too close to it. Step back a little.'

'Sure,' I agreed. 'The trouble is — '

A knock on the door interrupted me. I wasn't expecting anyone — certainly not the person who walked in a moment later.

Zelda Marshall closed the door quietly behind her and came to stand in front of the desk. She didn't look her usual self. There were dark circles under her eyes and she wore no lipstick.

'I think you'd better have a seat,' I said. 'Are you all right?'

Her lips twitched into what was intended to be a smile. 'Not really,' she replied. 'I just heard about Michael yesterday. Who could possibly want to kill him?'

She dabbed at her eyes with a handkerchief. 'I don't know what other people thought about him but he was good to me.'

'I'm sure he was,' I said. 'But why did

you discharge yourself from hospital and where the hell have you been these past few days? I think I should tell you that Lieutenant O'Leary has had men looking all over L.A. for you.'

'I guessed that might happen. That's why I went away for a few days to try to get my mind into some kind of order. When I woke in the hospital and was told that I'd been shot and that woman who was with me that night had been killed, I knew I had to get away.'

'So where did you go?' Dawn asked.

'I went back to Arizona to where I used to live before I came out here. I just wanted to get away from everything.'

'Can you tell me what happened that night after I took you to stay with Marla?'

She put up a hand to her forehead. 'Everything about that night seems just a vague blur. I know Marla remained in her chair after the lights were put out. She told me there was a bedroom upstairs but I thought it would be better to stay with her so I went to sleep in the chair.'

'Go on,' I prompted as she paused.

'I don't know what time it was, but it

must have been almost daylight when I woke suddenly. I had the feeling there was someone else in the room apart from Marla but I couldn't see anyone. Then Marla gave a sudden shout and made to get out of her chair. She had that gun in her hand.

'Then there was a shot from somewhere behind me and she fell back. I can't remember if I screamed. I think I turned to see where the shot had come from and then there was another shot. I don't remember anything more after that until I woke up in a hospital bed with my shoulder bandaged.'

'I see.'

'I really came here to apologize for all the trouble I've caused. I'm sorry about your friend, Marla. I suppose it was mainly my fault that she died.'

'These things happen,' I said. I didn't mean to sound callous but if it had been anyone's fault it had been mine for taking Zelda there and thinking I could outwit the Mobs.

'And what are you going to do now that Florencio is gone?' Dawn inquired. 'Are you going to continue running your boutiques — or are you going back to Arizona?'

The way she said it made me feel she was hoping it would be the latter.

Zelda smiled at that but it wasn't a nice smile. 'I've already made up my mind about that. You see, Michael and I had a business arrangement. If anything should happen to him, I take over the outfit.' Her voice was now like chipped ice. Gone were all the tears. I'd never seen such an abrupt change in a woman. She suddenly seemed a totally different person sitting there.

'If you've got that in mind — you're insane,' I said. 'Florencio's boys will never take orders from a woman.'

'Oh, I think they will when they hear what I have to say. It may surprise you but there are others who'll back me up.'

'Well I don't know who you have in mind but I don't think that Joe Malloy is going to stand by and allow you to have part of his Mob! Don't forget your boyfriend took orders from him. Are you willing to do the same?'

She laughed harshly 'Malloy's burnt

out. He's been in charge for far too long. I'll take care of him when the time comes. And you can take it from me that when I find out who killed Michael, he'll pay for it.'

Once she had gone I swung round in my chair to face Dawn. She looked as shocked as I was at what we'd just heard. 'You think she means it?' she asked.

'I not only think she means it, I think she believes she can do it. What worries me at the moment is this business deal she reckons she had with Florencio. He wasn't a fool and as far as I know he never went soft on any dame.'

I swung back to the desk. 'I reckon O'Leary has to know about this new development,' I said thinly. 'Not that he can do much about it. But it's my guess he'd better be prepared for an all-out gang war once Malloy and the other bosses hear about her plans.'

'And Manzelli?'

'I figure he knew about it before we did. He won't sit still either.'

I got O'Leary on the phone just as he was apparently going out. He didn't seem too pleased to get my call. 'I'm in a hurry, Merak,' he snarled. 'If you've got something to say spit it out and then get off the line.'

'I've just had a visit from Zelda Marshall, Lieutenant. Far from being the grieving widow, she's just informed me that, under some prior agreement she had with Florencio, she's taking over control of his outfit.'

'Like hell she is! Are you sure you heard her right?'

'Oh, I heard it all and I've got the feeling she's going through with it. I don't know what hold she had on Florencio or how she's going to sweet-talk the other members into following her. But I reckon you'd be wise take her seriously.'

'I'll take her seriously all right.' His voice was as rigid as an iron bar. 'Once I bring her in I'm charging her with first-degree murder. Then we'll see how well she can run that outfit from inside a prison cell.'

He slammed down the phone.

I could guess what the news had done to him. O'Leary was a straight cop who played it all by the book. But if everything did break wide open, he'd have both the Mayor and the D.A. down on his neck like a ton of bricks.

And you could add the Mobs to them if I was right and a gang war did break out.

That evening, once we'd closed up the office, I went along to the hospital to have a word with Sharky Dexter. I found him still in the same bed and still as angry as ever. He looked surprised to see me but waved a hand towards the bedside chair.

'Have the doctors told you how much longer you've to stay here, Sharky?' I asked, sitting down.

'They'll tell me nothing. Even if I did manage to get out of this bed, those two cops in the corridor outside wouldn't let me leave.'

'I guess that was Lieutenant Denman's doing?'

He looked momentarily surprised. 'Who the hell is Denman?'

'He's the cop who came just as we got you out of that office,' I told him. 'He asked a hell of a lot of questions. Maybe he figures you're still in danger from that arsonist. He's probably hoping the would-be killer will try again and he's using you as the bait.'

Dexter tried to shift himself into a more comfortable position in the bed, grimacing as he did so. 'Have you got any further towards finding that little guy who took me for a million?'

'So far there's no sign of him. He's gone to earth somewhere and you know how many places there are in the city where he can hide.'

'I don't give a damn about that and I don't want any more excuses. Just find him.'

'All right, Sharky. I'll do that.' I got up and paused at the door. Turning, I looked straight at him. 'Just one thing before I leave. That scam at the roulette table — were you and this little guy working it together to make sure the ball landed on number thirteen three times?'

I thought he was going to have a stroke. His face turned a deep purple and he seemed to be having difficulty swallowing. The next moment he had thrown aside the sheets and lunged for me.

Turning quickly, I stepped into the

corridor. There was a nurse coming towards me. Stopping her, I said gravely, 'I think the patient in that private ward is having a fit of some kind. He doesn't look too good. I reckon you'd better get the doctor at once to take a look at him.'

She hurried into the room and I left the building. That look on Dexter's face when I'd accused him of working in cahoots with Karmov had told me everything I wanted to know. That was exactly how it had happened. I'd been absolutely right.

Going out into the hospital car park, I opened the door of the Merc and slid behind the wheel, pushing the key into the ignition. Before I could turn it, however, something cold and metallic made contact with the back of my neck.

A voice I recognized at once said, 'Don't make any funny moves, Merak, or my companion will be forced to pull the trigger of that gun.'

'Just what is this, Joe?' I asked, swallowing hard. 'If you've got some beef with me, I — '

'Shut up and listen. I've got no beef

with you but I do want some information. I suggest you answer my questions and they'd better be the truth, otherwise — '

I kept my head very still as the gun muzzle was thrust even harder against my neck. 'What is it you want to know?'

'That's better. Now Johnny, I'm hearing strange stories about this dame, Zelda Marshall. I think you know what I'm talking about since she was in your office only a little while ago. What exactly did she tell you?'

I swallowed hard. 'She said something about a business deal she'd made with Michael Florencio. Seems that if he met with an unfortunate accident, he wanted her to take over his mob.'

Malloy was silent for a full minute. I guess he could scarcely take in what I'd told him. I knew his mind was working overtime probing all of the ramifications of this information. Finally, he said harshly, 'If that dame thinks she can muscle in on part of my organization she's a dead duck.'

'I didn't think you'd take it lying down, Joe,' I said.

'Too damned right I won't. Any of my boys who go over to her will end up at the bottom of the Pacific.'

'Do you mind if I ask you a question, Joe?'

'What is it?'

'Florencio was one of your men. Do you have any idea what kind of hold this dame might have had over him? It wasn't like Florencio to make any deal like that with any dame.'

'I've got my own theory about that, Merak.'

'Do you mind telling me what that is?'

He hesitated, then said tersely, 'Florencio was a fool where gambling was concerned. He owed a hell of a lot of dough to certain people in the Organization — important people. Some of them were getting a little impatient. But when it came down to hard facts that dame had a lot more money than he did. My guess is that he needed a lot of dough in a hurry and she was the only one he could get it from.

'There was also one other reason, one few people knew about. The damned fool married the dame in some place back east about a year ago!'

I forgot about the gun at my head at that bit of information and swung round to stare at him. One look at his face told me he wasn't lying. It was certainly something I'd never considered. In part, however, it explained why he had been so keen to get rid of Dawn and myself, particularly when he thought I'd insulted Zelda.

'Well, I guess that answers quite a few things that have been puzzling me,' I said evenly. 'But do you mind taking that gun out of my back? I think a lot better without that.'

There was a brief pause. Then Malloy said tightly, 'Put the gun away, Carl. Somehow, I don't think we'll have any trouble from Mister Merak. Now we come to the reason why you're here. Do you know where Zelda is now?'

'Have you tried Florencio's place? My guess would be that if she's planning to take that outfit over, she'll have to talk with the boys. Maybe some of them will go for her. My guess is most of them won't.'

I could almost hear the cogs spinning inside Malloy's head. Finally, he said, 'That's the way I see it but anything's possible, I guess, where that woman is concerned. All right, Merak, I reckon you're in the clear. Just make sure that from now on you keep your nose out of my business. And if you should run into Zelda, be sure that I know about it first. That's all.'

They got out and I saw them walk to the other side of the car park. I waited until the black limousine had gone before turning the key in the ignition. Those little mice inside my head were really enjoying themselves now, nibbling at the edges of my mind. Evidently there was a lot more to this Zelda dame than I'd previously imagined.

But even with all of the new information I'd gained from Malloy and my talk with Dexter, I was still no nearer to guessing who the killer was. There were so many loose ends still hanging out it would be easy to trip over them if I wasn't careful. I felt like a guy with a white stick fumbling around in the dark.

I decided I needed a drink. It would either clear my head or I'd sink into a haze where nothing mattered.

Mancini's was open as always. I wondered if it ever closed. The usual clientele was present, some standing or sitting at the bar, others seated at the small number of tables. I picked out a vacant stool and ordered a whiskey.

I was just sipping my drink when who should come along behind the bar but Mancini himself. It was almost unknown for him to work there but he now wore a white apron and looked as though, for one time in his life, he was actually enjoying himself.

'Ah, Johnny,' he said, leaning his elbows on the bar in front of me. 'I was hoping you'd drop in tonight. Jack Kolowinski was in about half an hour ago looking for you.'

'Oh — did he say why?'

'No. But he said if I was to see you to tell you he'll be back in half an hour. That was about twenty minutes ago. He should be here soon.'

'Thanks. Get me another drink and I'll

wait for him.' I'd no idea why Kolowinski wanted to see me but he usually imparted bits of important information that often proved useful.

He came in ten minutes later and I could see he'd visited some other bar on the way. One of these days if a slug didn't get him, the booze would. I'd often thought it was a pity he didn't have a wife to keep him on the straight and narrow.

'You wanted to see me, Jack,' I said as he seated himself on the stool beside me. Against my better judgment, I ordered a drink for him and waited until Mancini had put it down in front of him.

'O'Leary is as mad as hell Johnny. I was glad to finish my shift and get away from him.'

'Is he ever anything else? What is it this time?'

Kolowinski tossed half of his drink back, grimaced a little and then said, slurring his words a little, 'It's this dame, Zelda Marshall. He went out to the Florencio place a couple of hours ago. He said he had more than enough evidence to pin a charge of first-degree murder on her.'

'And did he?'

'What do you think? She had some slick lawyer named Ed Clayton who claimed she wasn't within a couple of hundred miles of L.A. when Florencio was shot.'

'That's what she told me,' I said.

'And you believe her?'

I started on the second drink I'd ordered. 'To be honest, Jack, I don't know what I believe any more. This damned case gets screwier every day.'

Jack downed the last of his drink and placed it on the bar where I could see it. I ordered him another but I hoped he would go steady with them. I wanted him to be talking to me from a vertical position and not a horizontal one.

'Have you got anything else you can tell me, Jack? As you know, not a word of this goes back to O'Leary.'

Without answering, he took a folded newspaper from his pocket and placed it on the bar in front of me. His forefinger jabbed at an item halfway down the page.

I held the paper up to what little light there was in the room. The piece of news bore the small headline: *Private Helicopter Crashes Into Sea.*

I read through it twice and each time the icy tingle brushing along my spine grew more pronounced. A private helicopter had mysteriously crashed into the ocean killing the pilot and a single passenger. It was believed the aircraft was on a flight from somewhere south of Los Angeles to an unknown destination in South America.

The two bodies had been picked up from the sea by a passing trawler. No information as to the identity of the passenger had, as yet, been released. He was described as a small man in his seventies. A case containing almost a million dollars in US currency was also recovered from the area.

As yet no information had been released concerning the cause of the crash although two members of the crew on board the trawler claimed to have heard an explosion shortly before they found the two bodies and the wreckage

'I figured you might be interested in that,' Kolowinski said, replacing the newspaper in his pocket. 'I think we can both figure out who he was.'

'Igor Karmov,' I said thinly. 'So he never made it to his new life.'

'You think it was an accident — or something else?'

'It was no accident, Jack. The Organization is too powerful for anyone to get away from it. He tried to steal a million dollars of their dough but he should have known he'd never get away with it.'

I finished my drink and left him staring down at his. As always when he'd had a little too much, he seemed lost in some private hell of his own. The booze wouldn't help him to drive his private demons away but I hoped it would let him live long enough to collect his pension.

The next morning I was a little late getting to the office. I'd had a sleepless night. My mind wouldn't let me rest. It kept coming up with questions, going over and over the information I already had, as if I were on some kind of treadmill.

Dawn was already there having let

herself in with her key. Even before I sat down, she placed a cup of hot coffee in front of me. 'You look as if you need this,' she said. 'What happened last night and don't tell me you were sober all the time.'

'Not all the time,' I replied. 'In fact I learned quite a lot of things I didn't know before.'

'Such as?'

'Firstly, it seems Zelda Marshall was married to Florencio. The marriage ceremony took place somewhere back east. That's why we never made the connection. Secondly, I asked Dexter outright if he was in with Karmov when that scam was pulled. He made a big show of denying it, of course.'

'But he was lying?'

'I'd stake Lieutenant O'Leary's life on it,' I said wryly. 'I also bumped into Jack Kolowinski. He reckons O'Leary is spitting nails because Zelda has an alibi for the time of Florencio's murder. Some lawyer she's hired is willing to testify she wasn't within a hundred miles of here when it happened.'

Finishing my coffee, I pushed the cup

away and it was at that moment that another thought struck me. 'I'd like you to do something for me, Dawn.'

She looked up, surprised. 'Sure. What is it?'

'The way the Organization runs its various outfits. I happen to know that quite a slice of any profits they make goes directly to Manzelli. But sometimes, one of these groups will make a really big loss, just as Dexter did at the roulette table. I need to know if anyone makes good such a loss — and in particular, if that someone is Manzelli.'

Dawn looked doubtful. 'And how can we do that?'

'There's only one way. I need you to quiz Dexter. As far as I know he's still in the hospital.'

The look of doubt on her face grew deeper. 'You think he'll tell me that?'

'I think he might let something drop if you were to use your womanly charms on him.'

I could see she didn't particularly like the idea. Dexter wasn't exactly her choice of a man to flatter. Finally, however, she nodded reluctantly. 'All right, Johnny, I'll try.'

'Just keep telling him what a great guy he is. My guess is that he's a sucker where beautiful woman are concerned.'

'And what are you going to do?'

'I'm going to try to find out more about this lawyer who's provided Zelda with her alibi. To be quite honest, I think it's got more holes in it than a pair of nylons.'

* * *

Half an hour later I was in the office of Harry Waldon. Harry was an attorney of some years standing in L.A. and also well in with the D.A. I'd known him for a couple of years ever since I'd left the Mobs and gone legit. His secretary told me he was out for an early lunch but I could wait for him to return if I wished.

I did. I seated myself in one of the chairs against the wall. In between phone calls, the secretary filed her nails to pass the time.

Harry came in fifteen minutes later. He

looked surprised to see me sitting there. 'Johnny! Don't tell me you need my services.'

'No just a little information, Harry. It could be important.'

'Come inside the office and tell me about it.' He opened the office door and ushered me inside, closing the door behind him. 'Have a seat, Johnny. You say this could be important so I gather it's something to do with a case you're working on.'

'That's right. Can you tell me anything about a lawyer called Clayton — Ed Clayton?'

Harry pursed his lips; then shook his head. 'Can't say I've heard of him. Does he practise here in L.A?'

'To be quite honest, I'm not sure where he has his practice — or whether he really has one. Though if I were to make a guess I'd say Arizona. That's where a one-time client of mine came from.'

Harry's eyebrows shot up at that remark. 'You think he could be a phoney?'

'It's possible. That's why I've come to

you. Do you have any way of telling whether someone practising as an attorney is what they say they are?'

'It won't take me long to find out.' He reached for the phone and dialled a number. He spoke for several minutes to someone on the other end of the line and then put the phone down.

'It would seem, Johnny, that your suspicions could be well-founded. My friend has confirmed that no one by the name of Ed Clayton is licensed to practice in Arizona. If you want my professional opinion, I'd say this guy is a phoney.'

'Thanks, Harry. That's all I wanted to know. You've been very helpul.'

'Anytime, Johnny. And don't stay out of touch for so long next time.'

'I won't.'

When I left I had the feeling that, for the first time, I was really getting somewhere. Dawn was still out when I got back to the office. While waiting for her, I busied myself jotting down everything that had happened since Sharky Dexter had asked me to find Igor

Karmov. The jigsaw was now being slowly filled in but there were still pieces that didn't seem to fit.

It was almost half an hour before Dawn returned. I lit a cigarette and waited for her to tell me what she had found. Opening her pad, she read through it for a moment and then said, 'I've managed to get something out of Dexter. I'm not sure whether he was telling me the exact truth but I suppose we'll have to take it at its face value.'

'Go on.'

'You were right about every outfit paying Manzelli a percentage of their profits. Some of them apparently don't like it but there's nothing they can do about it.'

'And if they make a big loss? What happens then?'

'Then it seems that it's Manzelli who has to come good for the loss.'

'Manzelli himself?'

'So Dexter maintains.' She closed her pad.

'Then that explains almost everything.' The bits were now falling into place in my mind. None of these killings and attempted murders was unconnected. They were all aimed at one man — Enrico Manzelli.

'What are you thinking, Johnny? You look serious.' Dawn came over and sat on the edge of the desk, one hand on my shoulder.

'It's all beginning to make sense now. I'd completely forgotten the most important bit of information we had.'

'What was that?' she asked.

'The witness who saw Sergei Karmov arguing violently with a woman not long before he died.'

'But can you prove any of this?'

'Maybe not. But if I can get all of the players in this little game together, face to face, they might just talk themselves into the chair.'

I made a couple of phone calls. Neither of the people I spoke to were eager to meet me but after a lot of persuasion I got them to agree to come along to the Comero Restaurant in half an hour's time.

As I got up Dawn said, 'Let me come

with you, Johnny. I've got a funny feeling about this.'

'Sorry, Dawn, but this is one time when I have to do it my way — alone. I couldn't do it if I had to worry about you all the time. These people play for keeps and they'd have no hesitation putting a slug into you — or having you beaten into a senseless pulp.'

'They don't scare me,' she retorted defiantly.

'Then they should. Because one of them is a vicious, ruthless killer who's already killed several people, sometimes for no reason at all, just for the sheer hell of it.'

9

Deadly Finale

Before leaving for the Comero, I made one final telephone call. It was the most important one. I knew that where this guy was concerned I was taking a big chance. The people I was meeting were playing for high stakes and if anything went wrong my life would be hanging by a single thread. The weight of the .38 under my left arm gave me only a little reassurance.

Two large black limousines stood just outside the restaurant when I arrived. I parked the Merc some distance away and gave the surrounding area a quick once-over before crossing the street to the front entrance. I didn't want anyone else around except for those people I'd invited. After a moment's hesitation I pushed open the door and went inside.

A big guy, built like Fort Knox, stood

just inside the door. He caught my right arm and slid his hand inside my jacket removing the gun.

'There's no need for that,' I protested as he took away my gun. 'I thought we were all friends here.'

'We are, Merak. This is just insurance on my part.' Joe Malloy called from the far corner. 'We don't particularly want guns going off and disturbing the neighbours, do we? You'll get it back when you leave. That is, of course, if you can satisfactorily satisfy my curiosity as to why you've brought us all here. Otherwise, I'm afraid you might not leave.'

'Oh, I think I'll be able to do that,' I said smoothly. I walked over to where he was sitting with his back to the wall. There was one other gorilla sitting on his left. The guy at the door walked me over and then sat at his other side. He placed my gun down squarely in front of Malloy.

At the opposite side of the table, Zelda sat with her legs crossed demurely. She gave me a frosty smile that would have frozen Hell over.

I pulled over a chair, spun it round, and

sat with my elbows across the back. 'I'm glad you decided to come, Zelda,' I said. 'I'd have been very disappointed if you hadn't.'

'I'm here because I wanted to tell you myself that, with Joe's help, I'm now running Florencio's outfit.'

'Of course you are,' I said evenly. 'That was the main part of the plan from the very beginning.'

'Plan? What the hell are you talking about?' Malloy leaned forward, his face twisted into a scowl. His right hand reached out and fingered my gun. I knew he'd like nothing better than to pick it up and shoot me with it. But he was curious. He wanted to know just how much I'd figured out before he finished me.

'Oh come now, Joe. The time's past for playing games. I've managed to work it all out. The Grand Design. The big shakeup of the entire Organization in L.A. The plan to get rid of Enrico Manzelli as the Big Boss and put you in his place. Oh, I'm sure that Sam Rizzio won't go along with it. He hates your guts, Joe. You've known that for a long time. But I think you're now pretty sure that with Florencio's and Dexter's men backing you, any gang war will be short-lived and you can finish Rizzio off for good. That was the plan, wasn't it?'

'You seem to know far too much for your own good, Merak,' Malloy snapped.

Zelda interrupted him. 'Let him go on, Joe. It might be interesting to find out just how much he does know. He isn't going to spill it to anyone.'

I turned to face her. 'Oh, I think I know the whole story now, Zelda. Once I was brought into it, all of you fed me so many lies you almost had me fooled. But correct me if I'm wrong in any of the little details. The big idea, of course, was to get rid of Enrico Manzelli. So three of you worked out just how you were going to do it.'

'Three of us?' Malloy inquired.

I nodded. 'The unholy trio. You, Malloy, were to take Manzelli's place. Sharky Dexter was to run all of the casinos in the city. The third member was the ruthless killer who murdered anyone who stood in your way. That's you, Zelda!'

The smug look vanished from her face as if it had been wiped away with a cloth. 'You gave yourself away when you killed Marla. You shot her while she was asleep and then broke the door in from the outside, shot yourself in the shoulder, and then tossed away the .22 you took with you. You seem to be quite partial to .22s. But, of course, it's more the kind of weapon a woman would use rather than a man. We generally use .38s or perhaps a .45 Magnum.'

'You'll never be able to prove that,' she said acidly. Her face was now as stiff as granite.

'You forget I'd known Marla for years. If anyone tried to break in that door, they'd have had a slug in the heart before they took one step into the room. But I took you there and she never suspected you. However I guess I should start at the beginning when you three decided to make it appear that Manzelli was no longer fit to run the entire Organization.

'Dexter fixed it so that Igor Karmov would win all of that dough. But then the unexpected happened. The little guy double-crossed him and skipped with the loot. So he brought me into it. That was just a ruse to put me off the scent.

'Then, Joe, you sent your hired killer after him — Zelda here. But she shot the wrong man in Karmov's house before escaping through the back door. After that Igor's brother had to be eliminated because you were afraid Igor might have talked to him.'

Zelda forced a smile. 'And I suppose I also made that attempt on Dexter's life.'

'Yes, that's true, you did. Maybe the two of you figured he couldn't be trusted after his dough had been stolen and Manzelli had to make up the loss. I doubt if you were as glamorous as you are now when you went into his office, slugged him, started the fire and then left, locking the door behind you.'

I sat back, watching their faces. I knew what thoughts were running through their minds at that moment. I knew far too much and I wasn't going to be allowed to leave the restaurant alive. While they had my gun they were quite prepared to let me talk my head off.

'And you're saying that I killed Florencio while I was more than a hundred miles away. You forget my attorney can prove that.'

'I'm afraid I've checked on him, Zelda, and Ed Clayton is no more an attorney than I am. In fact he's as phoney as a nineteen dollar bill. None of his evidence would stand up in court.'

I knew from the expression on her face that this remark had hit home. 'You killed your husband — oh yes, I know you were married — so that you could take over his outfit with Joe's help.'

Malloy scraped back his chair. His right hand was in his pocket. When it came out there was a gun in it, one that was pointed straight at me. 'All right, Merak, I think you've said quite enough. The time for talking is over. Now you're finished.'

'Somehow, Malloy, I think you would be wise to put that gun down on the table. And that goes for the rest of you.' The voice came from the doorway leading into the kitchen at the rear.

The next moment a fat man waddled into the room. There was a gun in his hand and three men at his back. Even in the dimness, Enrico Manzelli made an impressive figure.

Malloy hesitated and then placed his weapon very slowly on the table in front of him next to mine. 'None of this is true, Enrico,' he stammered. 'This guy Merak has invented all of this to save his own skin.'

'On the contrary, Joe, I believe every word he says. Now I'm not going to shoot you here although I really should consider it. You're all going to get into that first limousine outside and drive away. Do you all understand?'

There was no argument. Not that I expected any. With Manzelli, you either did what he said — or died. One after the other they filed out with Zelda in the lead. Two of Manzelli's men went with them to make sure they did exactly as they had been told. A moment later I heard the car drive off.

'Do you reckon that was wise?' I asked. 'They might still cause trouble.'

Manzelli smiled. It was not a nice smile, rather like one you would expect on the face of a tiger surveying its meal. 'Somehow, I doubt if they will get very far,' he said smoothly. 'You've done me a very great service, Merak,' he went on. 'I won't forget this. But now I suggest you take your gun, return to your office, and consider this case closed.'

I guessed that was as much thanks as I would get from a man like him. But in the circumstances it was enough.

Dawn was in the office when I arrived twenty minutes later. She looked at me with an inquiring expression in her eyes.

'It's all over,' I told her. I wanted to say something more but at that moment the phone shrilled. It was O'Leary.

'Are you ever in your office, Merak?' he demanded. 'I've been trying to get you for the past ten minutes.'

'Why? Has something important happened?' I asked innocently.

'I guess you could say that. Sharky Dexter just died in hospital. A sudden relapse according to the doctor.'

'Well I suppose that happens sometimes.'

'Not only that. I've just received a call

from one of my men. It seems this car, a black limousine, skidded off the road without any reason and smashed into a wall. There were four occupants. All of them were killed outright.'

'Zelda Florencio, Joe Malloy and two of his boys,' I said.

There was a pause and then, 'How the hell did you know that?'

'I guess I must be psychic, Lieutenant,' I said.

'Like hell you are!' he retorted. He slammed the phone down.

THE END